I0692165

CRUISING THE COAST OF NOSTALGIA

MAXIM JAKUBOWSKI

TERMINAL
PRESS

Cruising The Coast of Nostalgia

ISBN: 978-1-990682-14-8

First Edition

Published By
THE TERMINAL PRESS
Powell River, BC, Canada

Visit us: www.facebook.com/theterminalpress

CONTENTS

OLYMPIA EXPRESS

I was on a mission.

In the distance where the sea and the sky imperceptibly merged, the clouds settled like a spreading bruise of a mountain range on the horizon. The boat swung from side to side as it hopscotched across the rise of the waves and nausea swung like a pendulum between my guts and the back of my mouth.

I knew I was about to be sick and was unsure if had time enough to run from the safety of the Captain's Lounge through the swing doors to the deck where I could vomit into the beckoning sea.

JGB would never know, one way or the other, if I spewed inside the boat or outside, anyway. Why should he? It wouldn't affect the mission.

I ran.

Past the doors, the wind rushed against me, cold and bitter wet, a curtain of rain and sea, a lashing of elements that only served to make me stumble from one foot to another as I fought my way through the living waterfall to the rhythm of my bile rising up through internal parts of my anatomy I never knew I had.

Holding back my breath and whatever was already filling up my mouth fast, I ran, slid and hobbled to the railing, leaned over and, with a terrible sigh of relief, opened my mouth and allowed the vomit to evacuate my body. Only for the fierce wind that I hadn't taken into consideration to slap it back right into my face and spread the muck across my glasses, cheeks, lips and chin.

I wiped it off as best I could with my sleeve, disgusted by the smell, the lingering taste in my mouth and my sorry circumstances, looking around quickly to check no one had actually witnessed my discomfiture.

I made it back into the Captain's Lounge, where my small suitcase still sat under a wooden bench as I had abandoned it without a moment's thought as panic had taken over, the three green paperback volumes carefully wrapped inside pairs of black socks in a far corner of the beige suitcase which probably

WILLIAM BURROUGHS

THE
SOFT
MACHINE

n° 88

THE
TRAVELLER'S COMPANION
SERIES

now matched the colour of my face. I only ever wore black socks. Still do now, some fifty years later. A man of habit.

Two weeks earlier, the call had come from Mike Moorcock, enquiring when I was travelling back to London again.

"As it happens, in a fortnight," I'd told him. Some family obligation or plans to hunt down a handful of new albums which I couldn't get hold of in Paris or, at any rate, not at ridiculous import prices, or both, I no longer recall which.

"Can you do me a favour?"

"Of course."

"Jimmy Ballard has heard about some books; apparently they can only be got hold of in Paris. Was wondering whether you can bring a set over for him. Three books. And, if you could, I wouldn't mind a set myself. We'll pay you back, of course."

He described them to me and I quickly identified the books in question. Many of the bouquinistes with their stalls on either side of the river had piles of the instantly recognisable green-covered Olympia Press paperbacks. I'd always equated them with pornography and they had never evinced my interest. I was too young and too busy spending my Paris days and nights studiously looking for the real thing, that is girls who would be willing to sleep with me for love and not for money to have developed at this early stage of my life any appreciation for pornography. Just goes to show the vanity of youth!

Why would the admired and inspirational J.G. Ballard have any interest in dirty books, I wondered?

But I'd agreed to pick up two sets of the books in question by some guy called William Burroughs and bring them over to London when I visited next. "They're somewhat different," Mike had pointed out. "Intriguing, even."

So now I shivered in the boat's cafeteria nursing a glass of Tizer, sick like a sea of stars drying across my jacket, trousers and even shoes, smelling, no doubt, to high heaven, twitching nervously about my imminent walk through the customs shed upon disembarking and the knowledge of the books, which I'd since ascertained, were actually banned in the UK, clumsily concealed amidst my socks. Surely, secret agents hid their stuff in better places? If this was my introduction to a life of crime, it lacked elegance and wit, to say the least.

With a total lack of curiosity that amazes me to this day, I hadn't even glanced inside the actual books after purchasing them, with guilt written all over my face as if I'd been acquiring a stock of condoms, from the customary bouquiniste by the Pont des Arts where I normally obtained my imported Ace Doubles or Ballantine SF pulp paperbacks with Richard Powers or Emsh covers.

The storm abated as the boat arrived at Dover and slowly moored and the balancing came to a halt and my nausea receded.

Dilemma: should I rush off first or appear unhurried and isolated within the main throng of passengers? How should I compose my features to run the gauntlet of customs officers? How to avoid not appearing guilty?

I joined the queue. England looked grey as did all the other passengers surrounding me. Grey-skinned, grey-clothed, harbouring grey moods. This was, I think, 1962 or 1963. It would be a few more years before I could think of England in terms of actual colours. Even the white cliffs shared forty nine shades of grey.

Clutching my sole suitcase, fake-leather layer across rigid cardboard, the handle slippery or maybe it was my hand sweating.

Finally, the gangway.

Inching down towards terra firma, the humid stone of the dock crisscrossed by rail tracks. A procession to the main terminus building. A wave of lukewarm heat and smells of onion as the door opened.

Entering the Interzone.

The crowd parting in front of me. To the left, the red channel, to my right, green, 'nothing to declare'. I veered, accordingly, to the right.

The pace slowed and I couldn't see far ahead. My eyes focused on the ankles of the woman standing in the queue in front of me. Slender, sculpted, white-skinned, just a suspicion of bare flesh between her brown boots and the ridge of her green coat. A quick glance higher: she had red hair. My heart jumped with lust. Not the right moment.

We waited.

The queue ahead slowly crawled forward.

Time as a slow river.

The red-headed girl whose face I hadn't been able to make out moved away and it was my turn to pass by the desk. I handed over my battered blue passport. The immigration officer threw me a disinterested look, his mouth half-opened, making me think of fish gasping for air under water, but he closed it promptly and didn't ask me anything. I moved on.

A long corridor.

At its end, like an opening in the horizon of a tunnel, an exit door, like a window to freedom.

My pace quickened.

"Sir?"

I froze. Looked up. A uniformed customs official loomed over me.

"Me?"

"Yes, Sir... Would you mind coming over here?"

I tried to look as innocent as I could, without much success.

"I have nothing to declare," I stated, unemotionally, almost spelling out the words in an even manner.

He pointed to an office. Waved me ahead.

A small room, with photos of the Queen and the then previous Prime Minister hanging from the whitewashed walls.

A second officer who appeared to be his double, same uniform, similar height, equally foreboding, stood waiting and gave me the once over. Unlike his predecessor, however, he was armed, a sub-machine gun hanging from a strap on his shoulders, all the way down to mid-thigh. Its dull metal sheen swallowing all the light in the narrow room. sucking it out of the air, like a narrow tunnel bridging the short space between me, them and the naked light bulb hanging from the geographically precise centre of the ceiling.

Without specifically having been asked I set my small suitcase down on the desk and awaited their instructions or questions.

"Anything to declare, young Sir?" One of them asked.

His accent sounded incongruously Mexican. Which made no sense. But then neither did his weapon.

"No, nothing to declare," I repeated.

"Is that so?" said the other customs official, leering down at me, as if he could read my mind or X-raying straight past my clothing or the tenuous fabric of my piece of luggage all the way through my darned black socks and their illegal content.

"Hmm, hmm..." I opined.

"You are absolutely certain?" one of them insisted.

"I am."

"No cigarettes?"

"No. I don't smoke actually." Which was true.

"No booze?" he continued.

"I don't drink alcohol," I said. Which was again true. At the time, I mostly drank lemonade, but would, in later life, graduate on a grand scale to Coca Cola and later Pepsi Cola which I would prefer to the former because of its slight back flavour of citrus.

"A perfect young Sir, isn't he?" one of the officials said to the other.

"Surely, everyone has some vices," his counterpart responded. "So, what are your secrets, young Mr..." I handed over my passport, and he found it difficult to read out or pronounce my name.

"Well, I like books and..."

They both roared with laughter, as if it was the best joke they'd heard in ages.

I remained silent.

"Can you open your suitcase, Sir?"

It didn't lock, but I moved the catch and opened the suitcase wide. There wasn't much to see, a few shirts in dire need of ironing, a spare set of underwear, an actual few books, a notepad, a pair of shoes, my toiletry kit.

"Could you open up your shaving bag, Sir?" I was ordered.

I pulled on the zip.

One of them looked inside and saw nothing to alarm him.

"No fresh fruit?"

"What?"

"No fresh fruit, I asked…"

"No, none at all… Why?"

"No bananas?"

To say I was puzzled by the turn of events and enquiries would have been an understatement. Bananas? Where? Why? An ironic smile almost drew itself across my lips.

"No."

"So our young Sir hasn't any bananas?"

"No."

They both closed in on me, crowding me, pouring with menace."

"Pass that shaving bag over, would you?"

I obeyed.

One of the uniformed officials, who now appeared to be growing taller and broader with every passing second, pulled out my tube of Colgate toothpaste from the kit. Unscrewed it.

"Are you absolutely certain you have no bananas?"

"Of course."

Maybe it was a Spanish accent, not a Mexican one.

He then squeezed the tube and the white paste spurted out, falling across the table in slow motion like expelled sperm, missing my open suitcase by inches.

He dipped his finger in the paste and brought it to his nose. Sniffed. A look of disappointment spread across his pudgy features. Indeed, no bananas.

The two men looked at each other and I briefly thought I was about to be dismissed.

But a look of connivance circulated from brow to brow.

"According to the manual there are other reported methods for smuggling bananas, aren't there?"

'There are."

"Sir, could you strip?"

"Undress?"

"That's what I said."

"Here, right now?"

"Where else, would you prefer we escort you outside to the quay and get you to strip in the cold in front of the other voyagers?"

I hesitated.

"There are no rules to say we can't do that, you know." He patted the submachine gun against his thigh.

I undressed. One item at a time, I began with my coat. Followed by my shirt, my under-vest, then my trousers. Stopped. Looked up at the two men as if boasting there had been no bananas concealed in my clothing.

"So?"

"You mean...?"

"All the way, Young Sir. Shoes and socks first, thought, after all we need some decorum, don't we? Nothing more ridiculous than a grown man wearing socks, is there?"

I proceeded.

Soon, I stood there naked, under the persistence of their gaze.

"A bit skinny, no?"

"Must be Jewish, don't you think? He's cut..."

I blushed, following the direction of their stare.

"Oh, yes," the other officer continued to comment, "I see. Nice size, though, considering the cold. They always say they shrivel a little when exposed to the air..."

I was lost for words and reckoned it was for the best to remain silent. But at the back of my mind I was wondering who these guys were? Genuine customs inspectors? Pirates? Mad men? Has I landed inside a book of the type I read too many of?

One of the men swivelled round and posted himself behind me. I could smell his breath on my neck. He reeked of garlic and dry sweat.

The silence continued. My eyes were drawn to the gun the official facing me held, the elongated neck, the muzzle through which a blur of movement appeared to be forming. A cluster of bees? A colony of ants about to take flight? I blinked and the absurd vision disappeared just as if felt a hand slipping between my thighs and cupping my balls.

"What the..."

"Nothing there," the inspector standing behind me and examining me stated.

I gnashed my teeth. The cursive movement of his fingers on my testicles had initiated, much against my will, a physical reaction and I was beginning to harden.

"Oh, signs of life..." the official facing me remarked.

"Probably means he's innocent," the other said. "The guilty parties are normally too tense to react properly down there."

I tried to control my cock, to no avail. It rose slightly. Engorging. Avoided my interlocutor's eyes, experiencing a curious form of shame and what was anything but desire.

"Just one more thing, then," one of the men said.

I froze, guessing what the final part of the exam was just a fraction of a second before a dry finger forcefully breached my sphincter and delved inside my arsehole. Words died inside my throat.

The penetration lasted for what felt like an eternity, and then the digit finally withdrew and I experienced a sudden, dizzying form of dizziness. I avoided looking down at my penis, which I knew was fully erect.

"Nah. No bananas. Mind you, I think he's actually a virgin. So tight, the way he instinctively gripped on entry..." the examiner remarked.

There were so many things I wanted to say, to protest, but nothing could pass my parched lips, held back by a knot in my throat.

"I reckon we're done." The shadow of the inspector who had stood behind me and probed and touched me up ran against the opposing wall as his colleague negligently adjusted the strap of his weapon on his shoulders and stepped towards the door, where his companion promptly followed.

"Goodbye Sir. That will be all."

Their identical faces exchanged smiles and as they unlocked the door, their features appeared to melt into a puddle that briefly gelled into a deformed Lovecraft-like fuzzy monster of the deeps, lips pendulous, eyes bloodshot and deep set, chin liquefying, hair on fire like Medusa, only the uniforms and the machine gun conserving their original shape as my memory of them faded.

They left the room, leaving me alone and naked. I quickly snatched my clothing from the table where I had set it down and hurriedly dressed, still reeling from what had happened. I snapped my suitcase shut and rushed towards the door. As I did so, I noticed a small desk in a darkened far corner of the room on which an antique typewriter sat.

The keyboard rattled away, typing what looked like an official report, with no human hand on view. Just a bee or was it an ant running down the QWERTYUIOP corridor of letters and then back again and back again, like a hamster running a wheel.

I didn't linger and emerged into the corridor and, red-faced and anxious, merged back into the departing crowds from the ferry boat. Within seconds it all felt as if it had been a bad dream. I checked my watch. Barely five minutes had gone by. I hadn't missed the train I had a booking on. And the banned books were still safe inside my packed socks.

I stumbled down the narrow corridor, pulling my case behind me and I located my compartment halfway down the train. There was only one person already sitting there. The wheels of the train began moving, throwing me momentarily off balance. She was young, dark-haired, heavy fringe curtaining her pale forehead, pretty in a damaged sort of way. I nodded. She looked up from her French newspaper, *Le Parisien Libéré*.

"Bonjour."

She wore a black top which clung to her curves and a skirt with a Burberry checked pattern which finished at her knees. She'd tucked her feet in under her legs to sit in comfort.

This was how I first met Danielle.

She was a law student and within a few minutes her candour floored me totally. She informed me she was on her way to London to spend a week-end with her lover, an Indian doctor whom she'd been having a long distance relationship with for over two years now. And the way she described the sex they had made it sound unlike any I had ever had the opportunity to practice. Rough was the nearest term then at my still youthful and naive disposal. Naturally, I was all ears, images of lustful decadence unfolding behind the screen of my eyes with an intensity that connected with my deepest loins with a nagging sense of urgency.

The English countryside unfolded outside the compartment's window, green finally negating the overall greyness of the rural landscape and heavy sky. The doors to the corridor opened and a set of ticket inspectors stepped in.

"Tickets and reservations, please?"

They looked identical and my heart jumped. Could they be the same guys who had harassed me, humiliated me even at the customs point? Their uniforms were different and one of them was wearing open-toed sandals and no socks. And, this time, their accent was Germanic. His toe nails badly needed a trim. We handed over our documents. Mine were returned following a cursory glance but they kept on examining Danielle's ticket as if something about it was wrong.

"Any problem?" she asked.

"None than can't be resolved," the one on the left said, turning round to slide the doors to the compartment closed behind him. There was a moment's silence.

I came to my senses as they leered at the young woman.

"Who are you? Can I see your identification?"

They ignored my request.

"The system abhors irregularities," the official on the right stated. His colleague nodded approvingly. Again, he peered at Danielle's ticket and reservation slip. From where I sat it looked identical to mine. Quite normal.

"Listen..." I rose to my feet but felt a powerful shove to my shoulders that forced me down to my seat. "You can't just..."

A hand covered my mouth.

"If I were you I'd remain silent, Sir..." Saying this, he winked at me and I knew right there and then that these were the same men who had bullied me earlier in the customs area. The uniforms were different.

"After all, this could well turn out to your advantage..."

"Madam, these are forged. There is no doubt about it. None whatsoever."

I looked towards Danielle and the somewhat distraught

17

expression on her face confirmed the fact, as did her lack of protest. She looked down at the floor.

"There is no fooling the bureaucracy of the Interzone," one of the officials stated.

"So, young Sir, no bananas but now found consorting with dishonest individuals? You do get around, don't you?" They chortled.

They pulled the thin curtain across the door to the corridor so that no one might see in.

"I have an idea."

"Tell me?" the other said to his colleague.

"Could be fun..."

"And educational..."

"I'll pay her fine, " I offered, not that I had much cash on me at all, remembering the ordeal they had put me through earlier following the strip search, all in a spirit of gallantry I didn't know I had.

"We're not allowed to handle currency," one declared. "You just don't know where it's been, do you? Nasty stuff."

"So what can I do?"

I pictured Danielle being arrested when the train reached Victoria. Or worse.

"There's nothing you can do, young Sir."

"But maybe the young French lass could?"

I was perplexed.

I heard the sound of insects and threw a panicked glance at its point of origin. A swarm of bees was entering the compartment through a gap in the window that looked onto the rails and the countryside where a forlorn cow sat in splendid isolation between a web of fences. I blinked. When my eyes opened again, it was no longer bees, but a caravan of ants slithering down from the window sill towards the floor carpet. I wiped my eyes and the insects disappeared in a flash.

I looked up again and one of the officials was bending over Danielle and whispering into her ear. She nodded meekly.

They both took a step back to allow Danielle to rise to her feet, which she did then moved to face me, got down on her knees and extended her hands towards the belt of my trousers.

I sat motionless, holding my breath.

She unbuckled me and buried her long fingers inside my trousers and then delved expertly into my underpants. Then calmly took hold of my pulsing cock. And pulled it out. It unfurled of its own volition, as if disconnected from my brain or control.

"Ah... our little friend returns..."

"Oh, not so very little after all..."

Danielle lowered her lips towards my hardening penis and swiftly covered the glans with her soft, lipsticked lips. The sensation of warmth was overwhelming. Below her fringe, she looked up at me and winked complicitly.

It was the best blowjob I'd ever been given.

Although spoiled at times by the running commentary and lewd observations of the two Interzone officials watching.

It went on forever as Danielle applied her not inconsiderable skills to delaying the ultimate moment, by using tongue, teeth, lips and even throat—I had never been so deep inside a woman, or at any rate, my cock hadn't—to depths unfathomable.

When I finally came, the orgasm froze me to the spot, floating between life and death, wanting the moment to never end, anxious and fearful about the fall that would inevitably follow. I'd often heard the saying about dying and going to heaven and this was how it felt in the moment. Nothing else mattered. That this wasn't actually consensual, that we were being watched, humbled, displayed even.

I roared.

They sniggered.

I bucked.

They laughed.

I closed my eyes, surrendering myself to the grace of oblivion.

"They're gone. It's done." It was Danielle. She was still on her knees, wiping her mouth with a red handkerchief, my cock now detumescing fast. We were alone in the compartment.

I quickly fumbled with my crotch and slipped my wet cock back into my underclothing and pulled the belt tight as

I zipped up my trousers now peppered by the earlier stains of my vomit and now my drying semen.

For a brief moment, I just couldn't look Danielle in the eyes.

"It wasn't that bad, was it?" she asked.

"Hmmm.... no... not at all... it was..."

"Don't worry, it's not the end of the world."

"I suppose not."

"My fault after all. I shouldn't have taken the risk of using forgeries. Sometimes I take unnecessary risks. Just my nature."

"Do you?"

"Can I ask you a small favour now, though?"

"Anything. Really."

"I need to shoot up. All that stress. Just go stand by the door and hold it closed so no one else can come in."

"OK." I wasn't quite certain what she was on about.

She pulled a small rectangular metal container, not much larger than a glass case, from the voluminous canvas hand-all she had been keeping under her seat, opened it and placed the syringe, a ball of some brown goo, a Zippo lighter, a spoon and a large plastic belt across the banquette.

I watched open-eyed as she carefully went, stage by stage, through the process of injecting herself with heroin.

I had of course heard of it, read about it but never witnessed the act.

Later: "That just feels so good," her voice slowed down, languorous, lazy, relaxed.

"Was it heroin?"

"Yes, so much better than sex, you know."

I didn't wish to know.

"Have you done it often?"

I was meaning to ask if she was an addict. She was pale, but aside from that, looked like any young woman in her early twenties.

"No. It's expensive..."

"Where did you get the... stuff?"

"There's this cadaverous American medic, Dr. Seward, who practices from a hotel on the Left Bank, off the rue

Git-le-Coeur. I help him out sometimes and he gives me small quantities."

"You have sex with him?"

"No, he's not into that. He's pervy, but different kind of tastes. Also likes playing with guns in the Bois de Vincennes. I serve as look-out, or other things."

I confided in Danielle about the books I was smuggling into England, if only to demonstrate I was also something of an outlaw.

She laughed.

"A book smuggler! You should have worn a beret!"

Over the following years, whenever one of us would happen to be in be in each other's city. There was nothing exclusive about it, we weren't in love, more like fuck buddies, an expression that wouldn't come into its own until several decades later. The penultimate time I was in Paris, visiting from London, and she had long ago escaped the clutches of her Indian doctor and was studying to become a librarian. She had an apartment close to La Roquette, one of the main Paris prisons for women. We'd made sweaty love between dirty sheets and were dozing silently when her doorbell rang and another casual lover of hers turned up in search of similar sexual solace. She was a young woman who had always been generous with her favours. She'd suggested on the spot we have a threesome, as our own exertions had not either tired her out or satisfied her enough, but in a spirit of obtuseness which I regret to this day I had turned down this opportunity and remained in the bed we had just used and listened through what was left of the night to their acrobatic copulations in the nearby kitchen.

The final time I saw Danielle was in London where she rang me at work, desperate, broke, begging almost. Some guy or other she'd been with had thrown her out on the street. I was staying with my family at the time and couldn't bring her home, so after an Indian meal in Soho, we ended up in the cheapest hotel I could find at such a late hour and with limited cash in my wallet, where the night manager granted us access to a tiny room under the eaves off a square in Bloomsbury. It was sordid. I was sordid and talked her into having anal sex. I thrust so hard, knowing I was hurting her. But she didn't say a word. She looked thin, drawn, ill. Shamefully, I left in early morning leaving her alone in the room without a word of goodbye. She didn't have a penny to her name, just the clothes on her back, had to return to Paris within the next few days or she would be kicked off her course and had no ticket back. I couldn't help. Didn't want to help. I was frightened of her or what she now represented. Was unsure whether she was still using. I'm not proud of myself. I regret that night and morning to this day.

Many years later when I became familiar with the internet, I did a series of searches for her and was surprised to learn she was still alive and appeared to have made a life for herself in the law, and was even a minor celebrity there, having lectured on certain aspects of the legal process at a variety of universities and published papers. I did not try and make contact.

We exchanged telephone numbers and addresses at Victoria where the Indian medic awaited her. He was short and tubby and bald. Which made me intensely jealous. She went off on her quest for rough sin and I proceeded to Ladbroke Grove to give the books to Mike Moorcock.

Mission accomplished. My first brush with the dark world.

Some months later, I received one of Jimmy Ballard's handwritten letters thanking me profusely for having obtained the Burroughs trio of books for him, stating they had had a profound effect on him and his ways of thinking and writing. I hope that by the time he got them into his hands the smell of my old socks no longer rose from them odorously! As I doubt if my own books will survive the ravages of time, let literary fame cling to me feebly for having introduced the world of William S. Burroughs to J.G. Ballard, a fact since documented in his biography by John Baxter and extensive biographical papers by David Pringle!

Eventually, I would read Burroughs and found him provocative, fascinating but, as far as I was concerned, anything but life-changing. But then I would always be a man with slightly different vices, impervious to drugs, alcohol, tobacco et al, although partial to the curve of a woman's body, the taste of a female lip, the fractal geometry of her lines of desire, chocolate, Coca Cola and the mad accumulation of books, films and music. But who am I to judge if J.G. Ballard, Mike Moorcock and so many others and betters from the old New Worlds crew venerated him. I even met the man, when he 'performed' live at the Worthing Festival, with Jimmy dragged in to present him on stage between anonymous early 70s rock bands none of whom survived to tell the tale. He looked like death warmed up, was rude and his voice was a dry, unappealing rasp. So much for prophets!

I was once even offered the opportunity to publish his novel Cities of the Red Night when I ran Virgin Books, but was discouraged to do so by my sales team once they had checked on his previous publishing record. Of course, by then his books were no longer banned in Britain and were the object of a discrete cult. I probably still have my extensive set of Olympia Press green paperbacks on some shelf, but for years was distinctly more interested in the more openly erotic ones, as by then my own sex life had become distinctly more complicated.

But, on occasions, I still see the bees and the ants invading rooms, or dream of keyboards, and these days computer screens, supporting cavalcades of weird beasts. But it's my secret and even my closest remain in ignorance.

As for the inspectors, I would come across them again, but that's another story altogether, involving further humiliation, disgusting practices and contortions, orifices you don't want to think about, excess like you wouldn't believe and if that were to become public, I'd become an overnight pariah, so that's enough of a confession for one story.

THE BALLARDIANS

There was a war.

It was not between the rich or the poor. Nor between men and women. And it wasn't happening on land, whether in trenches or on a bloody battlefield.

It was a war at sea.

The conference had been organised by the University of Aberystwyth and would be taking place on the MV Columbus while cruising off French Polynesia. Some of the more eminent JGB specialists had been invited to debate and talk on aspects of their favourite subject and although many of them had a declared fear of sea sickness, the handsome fee on offer had prevailed. Amongst the speakers were Pringle, Self, McGrath, Sellars, Jakubowski, Vaughan, Baxter, Wilson and lesser lights in the complicated Ballard universe, including the actress Kara Unger who had featured prominently in David Cronenberg's adaptation of *Crash* for the big screen; the Canadian director had not been available or willing to participate in the symposium and the actor James Spader had conveyed his regrets, busy filming he latest series of *The Blacklist*, and unable to accept the invitation to participate and reminisce. Holly Hunter had, on the other hand, promptly declined the offer to be involved.

We embarked at the Swinford Street Los Angeles World Cruise Center by Long Beach on a Saturday morning, straight from the overnight airport chain hotel at LAX where visitors from Europe had been accommodated following their lengthy flights the previous day. My room on the 13th floor had from its dizzy height overlooked one of the actual runways, but the efficient soundproofing had shielded me from the rumbling of the planes below, and I slept like the proverbial log, waking up full of expectations and with a ferocious appetite which the extensive selection and variety at the breakfast buffet tables rewarded. I was well fed and raring to go by the time our transport arrived to take us the docks where, with a tinge of nervousness, I allowed one of the porters to carry my luggage which I was assured would be escorted straight to my cabin well before the boat sailed in mid-afternoon. I'd long, on my travels, suffered with acute paranoia at being parted from my suitcase, which had a singular habit in airport luggage halls of invariably being one of the final ones to arrive on the conveyor belt with my private thoughts moving rapidly into anxiety gear. On this occasion my fears were unjustified as my case arrived barely five minutes after the steward for that particular section of the corridor introduced me to the cabin and I had barely had time enough to jettison my jacket and freshen up. Maybe this was a good omen.

It was my first time on a cruise ship and what struck me first was how the long, seemingly endless corridors cutting through the interior of the vessel reminded me so strongly of Kubrick's *Overlook Hotel* scenes or the hallucinatory vistas of the blazing inferno in the Coen Bros' *Barton Fink*.

I was informed by the Sri Lankan steward that I was on Vasco De Gama deck. Each level on Columbus was named after a famous explorer, with the ship's crew billeted on Amundsen which appeared to sit under the waterline, and the top deck with the more expensive staterooms and suites being Marco Polo.

The symposium would stretch over three days. The organisers had arranged for each session to highlight one particular aspect of Ballard's work. The opening day would be devoted to swimming pools, the following to car crashes and the final session to urban warfare. In between each session there would be a day at sea and another where we would dock at, respectively, Nuku Hiva, Bora Bora and Tahiti, from where we would all be flown back to our countries of departure. Nine days with the Ballardians.

It was clear from the onset talking to participants and speakers at one of the boat's many bars—here again, in deference to the theme of the conference each one had been renamed after a place with a strong connection to JGB's work: Shanghai, Shepperton, Cannes and Eniwetok—that almost every one attending the symposium clearly belonged in a separate camp, according to their interpretation and the influence on their thinking of his books, much like the way the decks and bars of Columbus reflected preferences. As it was we were evenly distributed between the decks irrespective of what we felt was the most important aspect of the JGB *oeuvre*; it would have been ironic had we, in advance, been segregated into specific decks according to our leanings, like the societal strands in *High-Rise*.

After witnessing a major row at the Shanghai Bar on Livingston deck towards the end of the conference's first day of lectures and presentations between a group of French epistemologists arguing with vehemence that the geometrical angle of crushed car bonnets allied with the topography of motorways (or as some of American participants—a minority of the symposium audience, however—called highways) concealed a secret code that superseded the equation of swimming pool length over depth at the deep end in reaching a proper understanding of the JGB psyche, I came to the conclusion that academia was just going too far and regressing to infantilism. I much preferred the interventions by Pringle and Jakubowski which were of a more autobiographical nature and involved men who had actually known Ballard, and had a healthy disregard for algorithms and all that jazz.

I moved away from the crowded, animated bar and the increasingly heated conversations just as a Sao Paulo University researcher threw a half-full glass at his interlocutor, screaming "Go fuck your bloody swimming pool and see if you enjoy it!" The other man ducked and the contents of the glass splashed against a passing young woman's immaculately white dress and she shrieked in anger.

That's how the war between the Ballardian camps began.

That night, a group from one unknown faction sabotaged the pipes connecting the whole water supply and evacuation system on Magellan deck where a majority of the swimming pool proponents were lodged, causing a major disruption to the whole starboard corridor and forcing faecal matter to regurgitate upwards through the toilet bowls into most of the cabins.

I had no opinion in the disputes that were dangerously

getting out of hand. My personal sphere of interest was an almost forgotten short story of the revered author's called 'The Volcano Dances' about people fading into a tropical jungle, a tale full of extreme metaphors about the inner landscape, but also one that somehow connected to me in a deep way that I could not fully understand. I hadn't actually reread it in ages and was now unsure whether the story featured a volcano or not. At any rate, for weeks now, I had been constantly dreaming of volcanoes and been playing around with a story of a similar nature—plagiarism or bad influence?—in which a modern version of *Romeo and Juliet* in prose form climaxed with either the young man or the young woman throwing himself or herself down into the lava-bedecked mouth of the volcano, or both at the same time. Paradoxically, I identified with both characters and projected myself into their respective bodies as they tenderly made love. I felt the stab of his hard cock as he penetrated me swiftly on a bed of forest moss and, at the very same time, allowed my fingers, nerve endings in sensory overdrive, to lazily graze along the smooth surface of her breasts with exquisite slowness, counting the beats of her heart through the shattering whiteness of her skin, a sensation of pleasure which caused a knot to form in the pit of my stomach. I thus experienced both their orgasms and my mind blanked out for a second that felt endless and I woke in sweat from the fever dream of combined, exacerbated desire. As realisation dawned, I briefly came to the conclusion that I had lived through what it might truly feel to come in both a male and female body, or was it something else? Neither was it being on the conference boat that was responsible for these strange and erotic if highly personal dreams, as they had begun to seep through my consciousness months before my travel. But, to my disappointment, there were no papers at the conference about this particular story (there was one on record by a Canadian academic which I had browsed through years before but it had not left much of a lasting impression.)

The evening before we reached the island of Nuku Hiva, another serious affray occurred when a sudden but violent fist fight developed in the main restaurant, during which a couple

of dozen men and women actually came to physical blows over a further argument between opposing camps which flared up between the main course and dessert. As for me, I'd been eating at the buffet on the top deck as I was that evening in more of a mood for fresh air and informal attire. By the time the news reached me, it was unclear how the hostilities had begun or what specific contentious subject had triggered the affray. Half a dozen of those involved had to attend the boat's infirmary with cuts and bruises and, rumour was, in a couple of cases actual broken bones, but news of that kind in a closed environment like a cruise ship spreads like wildfire, with inaccuracies and disinformation growing with every repeat of the story. The all-female Hungarian string quartet who always played soothing classical tunes at the entrance of the large restaurant had, I heard, been caught up in the fight and one of their instruments had been badly damaged.

The following morning at breakfast, there was already a scattering of conference participants wearing specially printed T-shirts—made overnight by the boat's gift shop—declaring what camp the wearer sympathised with. 'Crash With Me', 'Empty My Pool', 'Inner=Winner', or 'I Have Faith in Dr Nathan' were some of the slogans on display. The way this was developing was worrying. What would happen next, I wondered, although at the back of my mind, I was still fixated on my Romeo and Juliet scenario in which the two sundered lovers each belonged to different, warring Ballardian camps. Ah, what Jimmy would have made of this!

"Did you hear?" Professor Kerans asked me as I stood by the juice dispenser waiting for my plastic cup to fill with grapefruit juice.

"Yesterday's fight? Yes, a few people have told me about it."

"No," he said, leaning confidentially against me. 'The aftermath..."

"Tell me."

"Rumour has it a Villefranche University female researcher was raped. Claims she woke up in her cabin, bruised and with obvious signs of violation. Someone slipped her some Rohypnol in her drink and must have taken advantage of her.

She can't remember anything beyond almost passing out at the Captain's Club bar and a man she had previously been quarrelling with helping her to her feet. All she recalled was that he was on the opposite side of the argument, not that she no longer had any notion of the subject they were arguing about. Some say he was a proponent of the wind sculptors of Vermilion Sands though..."

"Jesus!"

Waiting for the lift to return to my cabin, I could feel the tension in the air as other passengers surrounded me, people looking at each other sideways, with all sorts of resentment simmering under the surface. If looks could kill. As if, in some instances, accusing me of not having taken sides. The atmosphere was becoming poisonous. A good thing we had a day ahead with the opportunity to disembark from the boat's claustrophobic cloud of rising hostility. I hoped the skies of Polynesia would prove a soothing agent spreading some form of calm among our increasingly litigious crowd.

The only way to reach the shores of Nuku Hiva was by tender, as the island had no dock deep enough to accommodate a cruise ship the sheer size of Columbus.

Much of the island's natives were standing by the quay, wreathed in garlands of multicoloured flowers and playing local instruments in readiness to greet us visitors. It felt more like a museum display or some Disney movie, as we cautiously stepped off the tender and laid foot on dry land. Beyond the natives on cheerful display was an open air market with an abundance of trestle tables littered with trinkets, leather products, carved wooden objects and jewellery that looked as if it had sprung straight from the shelves of donated goods at Goodwill or Oxfam. Or maybe we conference participants were too cynical; at any rate, we were not the typical sort of customer a cruise ship would disgorge. I doubted the market traders would find today particularly lucrative. A small building with a thatched roof stood close to the improvised market and its rows of stools, advertising itself as both an information and tourist center and a museum of local history. Most of us bypassed the market and picked up local maps which were available for free.

In truth, there was it appeared little to see on Nuku Hiva unless you rented a car and drove into the interior, which none of us knew anything about, not having previously researched the island. The boat's shore team had not advertised any local excursions, a sign if any of the lack of tourist features of interest on Nuku Hiva.

On the tender, during the 15 minute journey from where Columbus had moored out in the bay and the small island, I had fallen into conversation with Sofia, an attractive young woman from Turin in Italy. She was not a Ballard specialist *per se*, but was working on a doctoral dissertation on David Foster Wallace and had generously been gifted the cruise by her thesis supervisor who had been obliged to drop out at the last minute because of a family illness. Sofia was into body art, so there was a remote connection to JGB through some of the more extreme developments in *Crash*, she claimed. At any rate, she quickly declared that she wasn't part of any of the opposing camps that were developing on board, and I reassured her that neither was I. More puzzled observers, we reckoned.

"Ha," she said, smiling. "So we're just voyeurs, spectators. Not in danger of stabbing each other in the back... Good!"

Sofia was both stick thin and busty, a curious combination that made her stand out in a crowd, with dark, thick curly hair held together like a crown high above her forehead. On her right temple, a patch of skin looked bruised or burned, signs of an ancient accident or a problem at birth. But, where others would have concealed this blemish by combing their hair across the stain, she proudly allowed it to be fully visible, almost displaying it with pride. Her eyes were black as coal and truly striking. She must have been in her mid-30s with sultry, angular Mediterranean features.

I was curious to ask her about body art, and conversely whether she actually had any piercings or tattoos herself, but in these awkward #MeToo days was hesitant to enquire in fear of taking that perilous step so far and not knowing her well enough at this stage. Ah, the perils of the new woke! Ballard would have found our times problematic had he lived on that long!

I came by Sofia again in the tourist office, as we both faced the counter and perused the brochures and paperwork on offer. We had parted at the shore where she had wanted to take photos of the natives in their flowery finery.

"Any plans?"

"No. Was thinking of looking out for a local grocery store or small supermarket. I need some bottles of mineral water for the cabin. At the bars on board it costs as much as wine!" I was lying: I actually needed some Cola, which was the only thing I drank in private. Water just had no taste!

"Good idea," Sofia said. "Can I join you?"

We were informed there was a store all the way further down the coastal road to the west, a twenty minutes walk away, where we would find basic essentials. The day was cloudy but warm, and we had little else to do. Most of the people who had disembarked from the ship also appeared to be heading in the same direction. We followed them at a distance. Many of the improvised groups still seemed to be in constant argument, arms waiving, heads shaking under the assault of rage, steps staccato to the rhythm of the heated conversations, dimmed voices ahead and behind us blanking out the sound of waves lapping on the shore, as if the literary war raging on Columbus had followed us all the way onto dry land.

Halfway to the store we were seeking the road briefly swerved away from the shore and a small commuter bus which had seen better days, its exhaust sputtering loudly along, drove past us, choking out a cloud of fumes. A wooden road sign offered us alternative directions: to the left 'Pirate's Cove' and further along to the right 'Tekoa Mountain' ten kilometres away. Sofia was Googling on her iPhone and informed me that Herman Melville had actually lived here at one stage when he was staying in the Marquesas Islands. And so had Robert Louis Stevenson.

As much as I was fascinated to lay eyes on the mountain which lay behind the Taipivai valley, equating it in my mind with the equally tectonic jungle landscape of 'The Volcano Dances', the idea of walking the whole distance was out of the question as we couldn't risk missing the last tender back to

Columbus advertised for 4pm. We made for the cove, treading unsteadily at times across the short grass and muddy terrain bordering the island's edge.

It wasn't much of a beach. A thin stretch of colourless sand, strewn with the occasional crushed, empty plastic bottle and wreaths of seaweed draped along a chessboard of grey and black pebbles. All it needed were the remains of military equipment or the charred metal ruins of a WW2 aircraft and it would have been properly Ballardian in its miserabilism. We waded our way through the detritus and reached the water line.

"I thought we might be able to swim," Sofia remarked. "But it's not very inviting." The ocean here, squeezed through rising verdant cliffs, was surprisingly grey, as was the sky peering down at us from above, and the nascent waves lacked any semblance of energy.

"I didn't bring anything to swim in along," I pointed out.

"Neither have I," Sofia said, with a twinkle in her eyes. "It's Polynesia, no? We could have gone naked?"

As much as the idea appealed, there was something about the way the landscape spoke to me that made a bout of skinny dipping unlikely. I pointed to a sign behind us, stuck in the sand, bending like a small tower of Pisa. It read 'Don't Feed the Sharks'. Sofia glanced at it and nervously laughed.

"Oh, OK..."

We heard sounds behind us and turned round to observe a group of half a dozen other passengers from the cruise making their way towards the narrow, abandoned beach,

'Terminal Beach?" a voice asked.

"You're a fool," another said.

"We should feed all the unbelievers to the sharks," one of them said, in a tone that sounded anything but ironic.

The woman in the group nodded.

"Who are these people?" I asked Sofia, whispering. I had not come across them at the conference.

"I think they're French," she said. 'They do take matters Ballardian rather seriously, in my opinion..."

As I watched them, the woman in the group began to

disrobe. She had been wearing jeans and a black T-shirt. She was middle-aged, full-figured and noticeably tall.

"No way there are sharks here, this ees bullshit," she claimed, pulling the tee above her head, her long blond hair falling down to her shoulders. She wasn't wearing a bra. None of her companions seemed to object or appeared to be worried about the warning panel that had been left on the beach.

As she slipped out of her jeans, I couldn't but notice, even at the distance Sofia and I were from them, that she had a small tattoo on her left buttock. An ace of spades. My mind raced. Memories of pornography past, or was it BDSM lore? A sign that branded the woman displaying it that she was owned or been bred and fully available to black men. Unpolitically correct again, but those sort of things stuck in my mind. I looked away as the woman shyly dipped her toe in the initially shallow water, and turned to Sofia and, again, the thought raced through my mind that with her expressed interest and research into body art, she must surely be pierced in intimate places too, or sport uncommon markings, but I didn't have the courage to ask her.

"Well," Sofia volunteered, "No way I'm joining her. It's not just warm enough, sharks or no sharks. Shall we go looking for that grocery store?" We left the beach.

We found the small supermarket at the intersection of the next two roads. We weren't the only arrivals seeking provisions and raiding the potato crisp and chocolate shelves. I located a 2lt Pepsi Cola bottle while Sofia purchased suntan lotion and cotton tips. Everyone was paying with credit cards, as we hadn't thought of obtaining local currency.

I could feel a quivering current of expectation racing between the young Italian woman and me, or was I imagining it, hoping against hope for a sexual connection? It was just something about the silences that separated us and the way this sensation echoed through the depth of her eyes whenever she turned round to face me. It made feel both on edge and excited.

'Time to go return to the war, no?"

We headed back.

We reached the tourist office *cum* museum well before the

departure of the final tender. We agreed to have a drink at the improvised bar that had been erected close to the tent where returning tourists could shield and rest while waiting for their transport back to Columbus.

In the distance we could see the tender vessel docking by the cruise ship a km or so in the distance where it was moored in the immense bay and emptying of its passengers through a large door cut into Columbus' side. It would return for us and any other stragglers in another half an hour.

A late afternoon sun was rising behind us above the stocky hills that overlooked the small port. Sofia had been wearing a loose plaid shirt above a white cotton camisole, and feeling the heat on the back of her neck unbuttoned her shirt and pulled it off, while holding her gin and tonic glass in her other hand. My eyes were drawn to her breasts as they pressed against the flimsy material. I gulped. There was no doubt about it. Her nipples were undoubtedly pierced. It caused a knot to rise in my throat. Either small studs or rings.

The ghost of a smile glimmered through the shape of her lips, as if she knew exactly what I was thinking (and seeing), and had only taken her plaid shirt off to tease me and was quietly pleased with my Pavlovian response.

I wanted to say something but was momentarily lost for words. When I opened my mouth next, the exact vocabulary had to emerge, or I would be forever burning my bridges. I took another leisurely sip of my *citron pressé* before setting the glass down on the wooden table.

There was a huge boom in the distance, its shattering sound carried through the air by the wind. We both looked away from each other and glanced at the cruise ship in the bay in the distance. A thin plume of dark smoke was rising from Columbus.

We froze in place, hypnotised by the sight, as were all the Nuku Hiva natives crowded around us, the singers and musicians who had been discarding their garlands and putting away their instruments and the market traders tidying up their trestle tables, packing up their wares until the next cruise ship arrived.

Not a word passed between us for a minute or so and then we witnessed a throne of flames engulfing the top deck, surrounding the majestic funnel, quickly spreading across the length of the boat. We saw forms, bodies, people, jumping from the top deck only to disappear in the waters below. bobbing along, flailing like corks or struggling to swim or float.

The quay was busy with voices and screams, but there was little anyone could do at this distance from the cruise ship and then a further two massive explosions detonated. A short while after as we kept on watching aghast with our mouths wide open, trying to absorb the terrible event, the ship broke up. Two or maybe three segments faded away from each other in the rising gloom of evening and smoke.

As Columbus began to list and sink, a mushroom-shaped cloud rose from the water as the flames consuming the vessel hit the sea, reminiscent in format of an atomic conflagration. Just as Ballard would have liked it.

Which camp had gone too far and was responsible for the destruction of the cruise ship in this extreme fashion no longer mattered. The war between the Ballardians had reached its climax and the world would never be the same again. It would be forever seen as the 9/11 of the literary world. There would be enquiries into who was responsible for setting off the bombs, although as there were several maybe there was more than a single culprit, evil minds sharing a similar, murderous idea.

And Sofia and I were seemingly the only survivors, stranded on a tropical island for now. Maybe tonight, wherever we would wearily lay down our heads, she would show me her piercings?

THE BEACH HUNTERS

Considering how much sex played a role in his life—having it, thinking of it, seeking it—it was a great irony that it just never occurred in his dreams. Nonetheless, those unwelcome night adventures of the mind were frequent and potent. Strictly speaking, the dreams were more like nightmares, but then he had never quite been able to make out the difference between the two states. All too often, he would wake up in the middle of darkness, his heart beating wildly, often drenched in sweat, stomach tied in knots, emerging from yet another dream riddled with anxiety, his thoughts racing in ever desperate circular motion, a loop he couldn't escape from, disturbing, gasping for air, his chest in a vice of oppression. He was already exhausted, both emotionally and physically, before he even rose out of bed.

The actual events making up the fabric of the dream would quickly dissipate, like clouds melting into the event horizon, but random, flickering images, emotions, fragments, feelings would linger for a short while and only later in the day would he recall some of the elements, the building blocks of the dreams.

Most of them, or at any rate the more, albeit briefly, memorable or affecting ones, involved beaches.

It made no sense. He was an urban sort of person at heart and beaches had never played an important part in his life: holidays in the sun, endless hours reading and tanning in the Languedoc, the Caribbean, Cancun or the Maldives.

And none of those real-life locales ever made an appearance in the theatre of his dreams. The settings for his panic dreams were generally anonymous, long tongues of sand, squashed between emerald seas and dense inner forests, mostly uninhabited, littered with seaweed, squashed plastic bottles, driftwood and the usual detritus washed in by the waves. Like a movie of desolation after the end of the world as we know it, dead landscapes draped beneath the ever-blue sky, silent, a stage for a movie still without a script, waiting for him to assemble the jigsaw that would make it complete, meaningful.

He was living with June Ann. She was a biochemist and researcher from New Orleans who had paid for her studies by posing nude for a variety of photographers which had led to a brief period as a fetish hard porn performer as Calabria Fortuna. Her notorious videos could still easily be found on the internet, and often while she was out working at her laboratory, dividing cells, and experimenting with seeds, he would indulge in the privacy of his study and linger guiltily on images, opened up to full screen on his desktop, of her being whipped, fisted, fucked by one or two men, nipples painfully clamped, clothes pegs attached to her labia, her full, heavy breasts swinging gently along with every thrust inside her, hypnotised as he was by the drama of super-endowed cocks entering all her holes, her mouth slobbering around them, and the indelible vision of her face covered in ejaculate, an enigmatic half-smile illuminating her lips while her eye-make-up ran dirty, smudged, destroyed, perishing across the beautiful pallor of her skin. He was in turn aroused by it and repulsed, ever trying to reconcile these snapshots of her past with what she was today, wearing large round goofy spectacles because of her short-sightedness, her long flowing hair no longer bleached to Marilyn-blonde extremes, cooking with healthy, organic ingredients in the kitchen, playing with her cats and dogs, as if the past was a different country and none of what she had willingly done, endured had ever happened, or surprisingly even left a visible scar, physically or mentally.

"How was your day?"

"The usual. Spent most of it behind the microscope. And the AC in the lab is still on the blink. We've complained to maintenance a few times, but they still haven't solved the problem. You?"

"I've almost completed the edits. Shouldn't take me more than a couple more days now, and I can move on to the next commission."

"Good."

He stared at her, yet again seeking out the invisible traces

40

of her past in her features, her demeanour. It was like an itch he couldn't help scratching away at.

She was arranging sunflowers in a vase, her back to him, the light from the window creating a halo around her head. As if sensing the insistence of his gaze, she turned round.

Their eyes met.

"What are you looking at like that?" she asked.

He looked away. "Nothing."

A pained silence spread across the kitchen.

"I know that expression," she said.

"No, really, it's nothing," he insisted.

As he said that, he remembered he had forgotten to delete the browsing history tabs on the computer, which she often used too, which would have betrayed the fact he had just a few hours ago watched the clips of June Ann having vigorous sex in every possible position with the dreadlocked black stud and the somewhat more innocent one of her fooling around in a hotel bed with another porn actress with an equally perfect body. The geometry of their interlinked limbs and parts like a new language, in high definition, every micro-dot of a goosebump on June Ann's then shaven pudenda in close-up like an extraordinary alien terrain of pornographic pixels, more detailed even than when he buried his face against her mound and licked her to completion on the now rare occasions they still fucked.

And although he had inevitably played with himself while viewing her old porno clips it wasn't so much the in your face obscenity of the terrible, repetitive penetrations that got him off, but the rare glimpses of her wide-eyed expression as waves of lust and pleasure washed over the screen of her features and she peered towards the camera as if seeking for something ineffable way beyond. Somehow, he would realise, some time later when they were no longer together, he was trying to discover how she actually felt, and in fact wanted to be her.

But then he had always had a complicated relationship with pornography, and living with a woman who had experienced its reality was creating a nexus of both desire and terrible vulnerability inside him.

It was curious that this didn't somehow express itself in his dreams, though, he reflected.

"I never know what you're thinking of," June Ann said, as she lined up the vegetables to be chopped for their dinner on the granite work counter.

He looked away.

Failed to respond.

"Maybe it's best I didn't," she concluded, lining up the spring onions and the mushrooms on the carving board and hunting for a large knife in one of the drawers by the hob.

Somehow neither said a word to each other that night until they fell asleep.

The beach returned in the screening room of his unconscious mind in the early hours of morning and he woke up, fingers gripping the edges of the sheet, vistas of sand like a flies in amber dominating the landscape, his body short of breath, his mouth dry and sweat pearling down his collar, the panic attack slowly fading as he heard June Ann's voice shouting out at him from the next room.

"You overslept and I didn't want to wake you up. I'm off to the lab. See you in the evening. Maybe we can eat out?" Then the sound of the front door slamming and her battered Prius crunching the gravel on the front drive of the house.

He looked at the ceiling, seeking out shapes, meaning. It remained blank.

Soon after that morning, he prepared a rucksack with spare clothing, and drove off. He didn't leave a note for June Ann in the way of apologies or explanation.

By the end of the day, he was several hundred miles away, two tanks of gas, a couple of chocolate bars and half a dozen cans of Pepsi to the better, already approaching the coast.

It was winter. Both the downcast sky and the sea conjugated shades of grey and he was sitting in a bar off the town's main promenade squeezed between bed and breakfasts, overlooking a pebble beach where only dog walkers and shell hunters walked at this time of morning.

The barman brought him his cup of chowder.

"It'll warm you up," he said.

"Thanks."

"It's better here in summer," the barman added, in a vain attempt to cheer him up. "Not tropical, but you know what I mean. We're not climate blessed down here. Don't get many visitors these days. Well, not at this time of year..."

He looked up at the man. He was in his fifties, his hair was thinning and his shirt had once been white.

"I think I knew that before I came to Van Demien's Land," he said, dipping his heavy silver spoon into the cup, stirring the thick, hot soup.

"So what brings you to these parts?"

"Travelling. Researching..."

"Really?"

"I read somewhere about Patagonia Beach and thought it would be interesting to go there."

The expression on the barman's face, as he rolled his eyes, was one of astonishment.

"Damn, I'm surprised anyone from outside the region would even know about that goddam place. Sure not a tourist hot spot," he indicated.

"There are stories."

"There sure are. I don't even know why it's even called a beach. No sand, just pebbles, rocks, waves. Centuries ago, it was said that pirates would light fires on the promontories to attract vessels into the shallows in the hope of shipwrecking them. And it's halfway round the world from actual Patagonia. Go figure!'

"I'm hoping to write a book on unusual beaches,' he replied, which was a total lie, a thought that just happened to cross his mind at the moment as he tasted the chowder which was much too salty and tasted more of potato than clams.

"Well, it's a couple of hours drive south. There won't be much traffic, I reckon."

"I'm in no rush. I'll get there some time," he said, concluding the conversation. It had been three months since he had walked out on June Ann and he had visited a dozen or so beaches so far, and still didn't know where was going or what he was actually seeking. It wasn't as if the sandy, blue-skied, coral beach of his past dreams could even be situated this far north, even if it existed anywhere but in his mind. But he was in no hurry. Since he had begun to travel, the circular nightmares and regular panic attacks had finally ceased and all he dreamed about now was women's bodies. He could live with that, although waking every morning with a raging erection made him feel like a hapless character in a Thomas Pynchon novel. It could be worse, he supposed.

He lingered in the town a further two days before he travelled to Patagonia Beach.

He arrived at dawn in the middle of a storm.

The rain was pelting down, playing a ballet of dissonances over the hood of his metal grey BMW, droplets skipping along in gay abandon like ants across an open fire. The wind had a sharp bite about it when he opened the door and he decided to remain inside the car until the weather calmed, even though his heating was on its last legs. He would have to find a garage soon, if he remained much longer in these inhospitable parts, and get it fixed.

By midday, the curtain of rain obscuring the beach and sea parted slightly.

The actual beach was narrow but deep, lengthy tongues of land venturing into the sea and its procession of high waves, as if probing the ocean's defences. There was a ragged beauty to the vista, a forlorn sense of brutality and desolation, an echo of the dead souls who had seemingly been shipwrecked here in times of old and witnessed their broken bodies washed onto the unyielding stony shore to be buffeted over and over again by the savagery of the waves.

The sky had cleared and was now the colour of washed out denim as he finally exited his car and stood on the edge of the small chalk cliff that towered over the beach. There was a red stain in the distance at the far end of the pebbled carpet separating the hills and the ocean. He peered ahead as the dot moved, slowly expanded, came into focus. He blinked.

A human silhouette bent over at the knees.

He made his way down to the beach. She was wearing a red plastic-like anorak and was scooping pebbles into a variety of small pails, marking each rescued stone with a thick marker pen in fluorescent ink. She saw him coming and looked up, her long, wet hair spilling from her hood.

"You're probably wondering what I'm doing?" she asked him, as he approached.

"Not so much what but why," he remarked.

Her smile was crooked, full of mischief.

"I'm a geologist. Taking samples," explaining herself and her presence here.

"It's a god-forsaken place to have to come and work," he told her.

"I go where the work is, where the beaches are," she acknowledged and stood up. She was half a head taller than him, green-eyed and wore no make up. "What about you?" Her skinny jeans adhered to her long legs.

"Just another beach hunter," he said. "We come in all sizes," he remarked.

"So you do." She set one of her pails down and advanced her hand. "Dr Trish Vaughan."

He extended his. Her handshake was firm and confident.

He introduced himself to her.

Later, he gave her a lift back to the small nearby town once they discovered they were staying in the same hotel. She'd walked all the way to Patagonia Beach, had to rely on local buses and trains. Trish was good company, and they shared a meal.

"What's your next port of call?" he asked her after she'd confessed her work on Patagonia Beach had come to its natural end.

"It's a resort on the west coast called Vermilion Sands. It was once a huge development but I understand it's fallen on hard times and most of the complex has been abandoned, and what's left of it in good enough nick has been turned into an artists' colony. There's been a lot of dredging in the sea nearby and the beach has allegedly acquired some interesting geological configurations through the redirection of the tides and the university have given me a brief to investigate further."

"How are you getting there?"

"About three trains I've calculated, and some lengthy pit stops if the time tables prove correct," Trish said.

"I'll drive you there," he offered. "I've nothing better to do and the place sounds fascinating."

"Are you sure?"

"Of course."

Dr Trish Vaughan accepted his offer. She also came to his room that night. Not that he was able to perform too well, his erections now somehow a thing of the past or consumed by his dreams and unable to repeat in the cold light of night. Neither did the fact that between embraces Dr Vaughan in all her nude splendour whispered in his ear that he should be rough with her and, *sotto voce*, even asked for him to hurt her. Trish observed his physiological and penile capitulation with scientific detachment.

To describe the resort as run down would have been an understatement. The tall, concrete towers which once housed thousands of sun-seeking holidaymakers in their architectural heyday were actually crumbling, roofs caved in, balconies detached from their facades or, in some instances, hanging precariously by an iron girder with countless shards

of masonry balancing above the void below, as if assaulted by some hurricane or typhoon just the day before, wounded giants standing blemished against the azure blue of the spring day.

The more exclusive stucco villas dotted between the Le Corbusier-styled towers were in better shape but far from habitable. There was no electricity, water, and mould and vegetation appeared to be winning the war, gradually wrapping the buildings in a thick, impenetrable coat of decay.

The dozens of Olympic-size swimming pools which had once been one of the resort's main attractions lay empty, scattered with detritus and the pitiful remains of dead animals causing the smell of decay to hang in the air. There was no sign of the artists who were allegedly active here.

As for the beach, it no longer existed at high tide, fully swallowed up by the encroaching sea and no more than a landing strip of damp sand when the waters retreated.

"There's nothing for me to do here," Dr Vaughan said, with a sigh of exasperation. "It's too late. Maybe a year ago or so, I would have been able to analyse the flows and counterflows of the tides through the stratas of the beach, but it's beyond repair, so to speak." It felt to him, as he looked out at the bruised landscape, that any trace of civilisation here couldn't have occurred here a year back, let alone a century ago.

"I wonder where all the supposed artists have gone?" There was no trace of their presence.

She gave a few calls.

"They left just a few weeks ago," she informed him. "I asked a friend in my department to look it up online. Seems they they've gone east seeking a volcano or something of the sort. It didn't make sense to me, some sort of psychic search. Not my area of expertise."

They drove back up the coast, mostly in silence.

Sometimes they stayed in small pensions and shared a room and a bed, but barely touched, sleeping in the warm glow of each other's body, content with just the companionship. On other occasions, they dozed in the car. His finances were running low and he knew that all too soon, his credit card would get declined down at a petrol station and that would be the end of the road. Trish was content to let him pay for gas and snacks, and didn't appear to be lush with funds either. Both travelled light, just a few spare clothes and some toiletry, and various small pieces of scientific apparatus in her bulging rucksack, test tubes, syringes, pipettes, multi-coloured sample cases.

They reached the Golden Littoral and Balmins Beach.

"Do you have any work to do here?" he asked her.

"No. My research is done. But I'm no rush to go home. There's not much waiting for me there," she said.

"Same here," he said.

"A few more beaches to explore then?' she suggested.

"Why not."

Balmins was rather notorious, not just a tourist hot spot, but also a gay haven and renowned for its isolated nude bathing area, situated between the glittering lights of the sea front promenade with its posh hotels and seafood restaurants, and the old port, which was now evolving into a somewhat exclusive marina for pleasure boats, many of which appeared to be owned by absent Russian oligarchs.

They were on their way back to the Port Hotel after a meal in the hills behind the beach, by the town cemetery, of grilled fish and polenta.

"I'm sorry," he said to her, "I like being with you but I'm also not a great social animal. Do I bore you?"

"Not at all. You're just a man of silences. I don't mind. I'd rather that than the opposite."

"You don't have to stay with me, you know. If you want some time off, feel free, no need to have me tagging along all the time."

She considered the offer and suggested she might go off on her own for a few hours, try a bar, a disco maybe. She felt like dancing. He agreed.

When she returned to their room hours later, well past midnight, she was not alone. The man escorting her was stocky, in his late 40s, he reckoned, impeccably dressed in a smart dark three piece pinstriped suit, looked a little like the actor Benicio del Torro, but without the sneer, not a dark hair out of place, ebony eyes, with an air of uncontested authority which hung above him like an aura.

He was sitting in the hotel room's only armchair, distractedly leafing through a foreign language magazine he couldn't understand, nursing a glass of water, when they arrived. Trish's face was blotchy, the alcohol she had imbibed betraying her excited state of mind.

"Who's this?" the stranger asked. "Your husband? Your boyfriend?"

"Just a friend," she answered boldly.

"Hmmm..." the man said. "I'm going to fuck her," he continued. "Do you want to leave or stay?" His tone of voice was full of impregnable confidence.

He felt a surge of adrenaline surge through his body, but before he could answer, or ask any questions, he was interrupted by Trish.

"I want him to stay, and watch," she said.

"If that's what you two want, that's what you will get," the man said. "But on my terms." He ordered the partly inebriated Dr Vaughan to sit on the edge of the bed and walked over to him, ordered him to rise from the armchair and stand by the far wall where he bound his hands tight with the belt he had deftly pulled from his jeans.

"Don't want any interruptions, or risk you having any second thoughts," he pointed out. "Just stand there and watch, or close your eyes if you prefer, but don't fucking move, understood?"

He nodded.

There was no fear, just a prurient curiosity and expectation.

"I think she wants you to see how she should be properly treated. Teach you, and her, a lesson."

The stranger quickly stripped Trisha and positioned her on all fours on the bed, undid his own trousers and roughly mounted her with no preliminaries. She moaned, and watching in dreadful fascination as he did he was unsure whether the sounds that escaped her lips were the product of pain or lust.

By morning, she had been used more than he ever

thought anyone could, soundly beaten, verbally abused, hurt and a parade of bruises was marked a crooked road across the geography of her pale skin, choke marks around her throat, broken in body and soul. But from the sketch of a smile birthing across her lips, blissfully content.

Standing, hands tied, by the wall just a pebble's throw away, he had watched in abominable fascination throughout, trying to understand, to process the events unfolding in front of him in all their crude horror, knowing that Trish was not just complicit in what was happening but also badly craved this repetitive pattern of degradation and humiliation.

'Benicio' left early in the morning, slamming the door behind him, not bothering to untie his wrists. He had to ask Dr Vaughan to drag herself off the bed, still reeking of sweat and sex, to do so.

She then moved to the bathroom, and stood silently in the shower, cleaning away the excesses of the night. No humming or singing.

She wouldn't look him in the eyes after she returned to the room.

"How did you find him?" he asked.

"He found me," she replied.

"Where?"

She didn't answer him directly. His eyes were drawn to the bruises on her small breasts, and the scarlet bite mark on her neck.

"Women like me," she said. "Some men, that type of man, they smell it on us, they see it even if it's invisible to others, the craving for submission. It's an illness and they are the doctors..."

"It's happened before?"

"Yes, an addiction, I know... but..."

He gazed at her. For a moment, he thought she was about to burst into tears.

"He wants me to go with him later, to the beach. He wishes to collar me..."

"Will you?'

"Maybe..."

After he walked down to the port to fetch some bread, jam and a bottle of mineral water, and returned to the hotel, she had gone. As had her rucksack.

He briefly thought, later that day, to amble down to the nude beach where the eastern quadrant was occupied by the gay community, with their tattoos and extravagant piercings and the 'free' area where all genders paraded as nature intended. But he did not do so. That night as he tried to sleep, he couldn't help imagining the stocky man brutally pulling a naked Dr Vaughan along the fine sand on a leash connected to a dog collar around her neck, her parts rouged, her eyes lowered as if in modesty, exhibiting her and then gifting her to other men in turn in full view of the whole beach and its denizens, before allowing her to be ritually devoured, consumed like in a Tennessee Williams play.

He departed Balmins the following day.

While the waves roared just a fifty metres away, he watched a group of locals kneeling in the sand, in a ceremony to honour the dead from the tsunami that had submerged the beach five years ago to the day. Their plaintive chant spiralled through the air, a sad lament orchestrated by a shaven-headed Buddhist monk in orange rags. The smell of incense reached his nostrils. The sound of tiny bells ringing.

Behind the beach halfway to the small road that traversed the village and its procession of bars, tailors and cheap bed & breakfast establishments, stood a rectangular granite monument on which the names of all the victims were carved. Next to it, a narrow canal serpentined its way across the back of the beach area, parallel to the shore, swollen once a day by refuse pouring down from the hills or dredging a torrent of mud after each rainfall.

A gaggle of street vendors littered the slightly elevated path that ran along the beach, hawking umbrellas, silk scarves, gaudy bikinis, and coconuts.

It was out of season on Tsunami Beach, still too close to the rainy season for the tourists to have arrived in droves. There was just a scattering of European retirees who enjoyed the clement weather and the depressed state of the local currency, and some gap year students seemingly all spat out from the same mould: identical dirty blonde hair, blue or grey eyes, sunken features, and on a continual high from the cheap and easily available grass.

He sat on the ledge, watching the waves break and a few tentative surfers treading gingerly with neither the talent nor the guts to tame them properly. Their boards were too new and their tan betrayed the fact they hadn't been around these parts for long.

"Just another fucking beach," he said quietly, with no one around to hear him.

Even the waves were nowhere like Bondi, but at least the place was cheap. His cash was running out, as were his options but he felt no desire to return home, to his own country, his old life.

He didn't think he could stay here much longer and realised he was overstaying his mental welcome. More than a month already. Time to move on.

He didn't even enjoy the heat that much.

"Do you have a light?"

Someone had sat down next to him, furtively, taking him by surprise.

"Sure." He pulled out his lighter.

In exchange, the newcomer offered him a hand-rolled cigarette and brought another to his chapped lips. They both took an initial puff. The stuff was strong, odorous. He'd never been particularly partial to it, but saw no point in being rude and refusing to partake. It wasn't as if he had any immediate plans and ending up high this evening wouldn't kill him, would it?

"I'm Kem."

"Kim?"

"No, Kem with an E."

"Ah."

Taking a closer look at his interlocutor, he realised it wasn't a teenager. He was older, grey hair flowing elegantly long down his shoulders, a bushy hipster beard moving between ginger and white covering the bottom half of his face. His shorts were washed out blue, his patterned Hawaian shirt a carnival of shells. His tan was deep, ingrained.

"Seen you sitting here a few days already?"

"Yes, I like to look at beaches."

"Don't blame you. There's nothing like the beach life, man."

"But I don't think I have yet found the right one, the perfect beach," he confessed, "Maybe I've been looking in the wrong places. Haven't tried any actual small islands yet. Might like them more. Commune with nature and all that. Earth, sea, sky, you know..."

He knew he was just spouting the sort of nonsense the guy would expect. Blame the potency of the grass.

"Ah, I know of a beach I'm sure you've never come across. A traveller's secret," Kem said.

"Tell me," he asked, if only to be polite.

"It's not easy to find, but if the stories are true, it's a hell of a place. Apparently, there's even a legend surrounding it. A hiding place, a base for the last mermaids remaining in this particular ocean."

"Mermaids?"

"Indeed. Did you know that no breasts feel as exhilarating to the touch as a mermaid's tits? It's unforgettable. Even a young virgin's buds aren't as magical, they say."

In truth, this was the first time in his life that mermaids had even neared the barbed wire fences of his imagination.

He briefly felt dizzy.

"It hasn't even got a name," Kem said. "They just call it the Final Beach."

"And how do I get there?" he asked his newly-acquired bearded companion.

His credit card was declined a hundred miles off the beach when he pulled into a gas station, so he'd had to abandon his car there and walk and hitch the rest of the way. It took him over a week. The road was a forgotten one, with barely any traffic, just a vehicle or two every hour.

He reached it at sunset, emerging from the trees that obscured the beach from the interior plains, the sharp orange orb of the sun sinking gracefully into the horizon, while storm clouds gathered above it.

His joints ached, he hadn't shaved in an eternity and must look like the parody of a caveman or a scarecrow, his clothes dusty, caked with sweat, his shoes falling apart with every new step.

It was just like his dream.

Desolate but beautiful in its loneliness. Empty.

He stepped out of his shoes, then his trousers, which he dropped to the floor of fine, yellow sand. He unbuttoned his once-pink shirt and pulled its starchy material off. Then his socks, and the glorious sensation of the unique texture of millions of grains burnished by an eternity of sea crunching under his bare feet.

He slid his boxer shorts down to his ankles and trampled them into the ground.

Took a deep breath and advanced towards the muted roar of the faraway waves, dipped his toes into the tepid water still harbouring the day's heat, advanced further until the sea reached upwards and submerged his cock, a dip in the sea floor and the water retreated upwards to his midriff, drops dripping from his navel across his pubic hair like a procession of pearls and then he continued his advance into the ocean.

His shoulders.

His neck.

His chin.

His eyes.

For a brief moment, he thought he should say something but nothing came to mind and he stepped forward until he was fully submerged.

And that was the end of that.

Later, the incoming tide would wash away the clothes he had left on the shore and there was no trace he had ever existed.

FIVE DESPATCHES
FROM THE DEEP END

1. ANNA X

Many years ago, during a fortnight's holiday in the Maldives, he'd written a whole short novel in part inspired by *Story Of O* in which the abecedary of BDSM was transformed by the existence of the then emerging Internet. Sales proved average, but a well-known Hollywood actress, whose backside in nude scenes he had long lusted after, had surprisingly acquired the film rights for a handsome sum, although the project never went into production. He was left with various editions of the book on his shelves, in diverse languages, all proclaiming 'soon to be a major movie' and with the money safely in the bank.

The story was about the travails of a married woman in Montreal whose life felt hollow and incomplete, who initially began trawling hotel bars near the airport in search of nameless hook ups. He somehow associated this with vague and possibly distorted memories of the movie that David Cronenberg made of *Crash*. Still yearning for more, the woman would eventually move on to more dangerous assignments of an extreme BDSM nature through anonymous contacts she would make online. The story unfolded through her email correspondence with a writer who lived in London who never either met her or found out what she looked like. The Internet handle she hid behind was Montana, after the American state.

Time passed and he found himself yet again trawling through the dark world that lurked ever invitingly behind his computer screen and came across a fetish website which piqued his curiosity. Skipping at random between successive links and revealing photographs he came across a member who called herself 'State of Montana' and allegedly lived in Antarctica (as all regulars of the site who preferred to remain partly anonymous did) and listed her age and gender as 100F, in a further attempt at protecting her identity. She stated she was a submissive in search of a master, according to her

profile and her mission statement and daily posted an artful photograph of herself, almost always in black and white. She claimed to be heteroflexible, a definition he hadn't come across before. A leg coated in pale, alabaster skin which through the miracles of perspective appeared endless; her pierced nipples; the intimate geography of her shapely perfect-sized breasts; her lips; the curve of her arse. Day by day, he mentally juggled all the photos she had posted and attempted to reconstitute the jigsaw puzzle of her appearance, but there were always pieces missing and there was no way of knowing the whole of her. Her hair was blond and unruly in an artful way, her corsets and lingerie lacy and expensive, and the collection of self-taken images all appeared to have been shot in a kitchen. Her classy shoes always had towering heels but somehow he could never fit all the parts together, missing a shoulder, her eyes, her genitalia (which she never revealed fully and always hid behind thin-fingered hands cupping her intimacy) and other elusive territories plucked from her private landscape. He reckoned a lot of other men around the world were also following her, similarly proving incapable of recreating her true portrait.

She was his character brought to life.

A woman he had created on the page who had now emerged into the world as a real person.

The fact she called herself Montana and quoted the title of his novel was too much of a coincidence. She must have read his book.

He was torn: should he send her a private message and reveal he was the man who wrote this book that now appeared to mean so much to her? Should he confess that her photos not only intrigued him but made him swell with desire? How can you communicate with a phantom?

He was acquainted with another writer who was not just a master of technology and the more arcane art of computing but also knew how to navigate the secret shores of the dark web. Through him he managed to obtain her IP and they narrowed her location down to Norway. Nothing more precise.

That same morning, she disappeared from the notorious

fetish website and all the wonderful photographs she had posted, beautiful exhibitionist that she was, had been deleted.

He was bereft.

Sorry he had somehow not downloaded all those enticing and provocative images she had dispersed across her page on the site, although he guessed, accurately, this would not have proven technically possible.

In his novel, Montana had also faded away, never to be heard of again. Another ghost in the folds of the Internet, leaving only bittersweet memories in her wake.

The following day, he bought a one-way flight to Oslo. He had no clue what he would do after landing at Gardermoen. Maybe Anna lived in Bergen, Stavanger or Trondheim? Like Montana, she might be married and just indulging her exhibitionist streak and not a deeper need. He didn't even speak a word of Norwegian.

Would he ever return to London?

It was like throwing the dice and hoping against hope it would fall flat with the right number on display.

2. KATE OGDEN

He received a letter out of the blue asking if he would answer questions about his translation of a strongly autobiographical French novel by a young, local graduate student. She was completing a Masters in Foreign languages and had somehow convinced Sussex University and its powers that be that disserting about the way different language translators handled the subject of sex in their work was sufficiently academic in nature. The book in question had been issued by his French publishers and he'd had the opportunity to see an advance copy and enjoyed it, and later convinced one of his English editors to licence the title and allow him to translate it.

The novel had been written by a then 20 year old young girl and unapologetically told of her past affair with a 50 year old surgeon who had groomed her. It was explicit, stylishly written, and rang uncomfortable bells with him as he had just emerged from an affair with a much younger Italian journalist which had left him bruised and hating himself.

He had trumpeted the book to Andreas, his editor, as the

flipside of *Lolita* and initially as he read it for the first time and later while he poured over its translation, it made him supremely uneasy as he couldn't avoid picturing himself in the role of the vile and cynical seducer. Add to this the fact that he had in between actually met Emma, the author, on the occasion of a visit to Paris where they had a coffee, and taken a great liking to her. The book became a *succès de scandale* in France, but had minimal impact in English though and Emma would only gain greater notoriety some years later with her third book which detailed how she worked as a prostitute in a Berlin brothel after moving to Germany and became something of a feminist manifesto. But that was later.

Emma had been flown over for the London launch and done an event at the London Review of Books store in Bloomsbury. He had noticed a pretty blonde in the small audience who, just as all the people connected with the book were about to leave for a pre-arranged dinner, had come over to him and asked for his email address. Her request for an interview about the translation reached him a few days later, explaining about her dissertation, which was titled 'Gender Perspectives; The Challenges of Translating the Language of Intimacy'.

He was happy to answer all of Kate's questions over a series of emails, and was later sent a copy of the thesis, glad to see that she rated his English version of Emma's book more favourably than its German counterpart, through his natural insistence on being less literal in an attempt to convey the emotions involved in a more flexible way.

He couldn't recall who asked who but they became friends on Facebook. She also moved to Europe, first to Brussels where she worked as an interpreter for the European Commission and later to Germany as a technical writer. He quickly came to believe she was gay as all the photos she posted were of herself with other young women, alongside plentiful images of herself travelling the Far East on a regular basis, lounging under waterfalls in Bali wasp-waisted in a luminescent white bikini, or wearing long, loose, colourful skirts in hotel lounges. He supposed it would be considered stalking as he on regular occasions trawled through her Facebook photo albums, but if there was a right etiquette to respect on the Internet, he was unaware of it and he carefully refrained from ever commenting on the images he spied. He often wondered how his old friend Jimmy Ballard would have written about the complex roads of the Internet had he lived long enough?

Some years later, Kate returned to the UK and suggested they maybe meet up for a drink in Central London where she was now working. He readily agreed.

Instead—he didn't drink—he invited her for dinner and they renewed acquaintance at a Mexican restaurant in Goodge Street. By now, his memories of Kate in the flesh had long faded and all he recalled were her photos on the Facebook page and he was surprised that she was so much taller than he remembered. He'd been harbouring an image of her for years as a pocket Venus.

Throughout the meal, and her complaints about her health (she suffered badly from endometriosis) and food allergies and bullying at work, he couldn't help but stare at her with lust, thinking guiltily that he must fuck her, bed her, mount her, love her, already thinking what the inner geometry of her delta would be like, the feel of her skin, the smell of her breath, the sounds she would make in the throes of sex.

They agreed to meet again.

They did so at his club, where she explained how her dating life had become a veritable wrecking field, and criticised most of the men she had previously slept with, emphasising how reluctant she was to go with men as old as he was, so the right moment for him to make a gentle pass never materialised. They remained in touch. She resigned from her job and was unemployed for several months. They would converse almost daily on WhatsApp and one day she hinted that, due to the poor state of her finances, she was contemplating logging on to a website where young women could sell their services as escorts for 'sugar daddies' or so-called mentors. They debated the pros and cons of the solution endlessly. He didn't want to appear pusillanimous nor encouraging either way and the matter was left hanging in the air.

The dilemma was whether he should avail himself of the opportunity. He could afford her, but would he be able to live with himself afterwards? Sometimes, modern life was something of an obstacle course.

Stuck in London due to Covid 19, he longed to be in the tropics again and wondered whether he might invite her on a holiday and take her to the ends of the world to some final beach somewhere. Paying for the vacation as opposed to handing over cash sounded like an acceptable compromise he could live with.

Tomorrow, he will ask her.

3. GIULIA DEZI

Giulia is in Manhattan, pinned down in the canyons between the Avenues where the wind blows hard, peering towards the sky that lurks above the skyscrapers, the uncountable high rises that dominate her present horizon.

Her married lover is at a meeting and she wanders up 6th waiting for him to be free.

Later they will return to the hotel where they will fuck again in the small room overlooking Washington Square until they are both dripping with sweat and sore from the friction between their parts, but ready for more the moment they cease, on the bed, on the floor, in the bath tub.

They will kiss, argue, embrace, fight. She wants him as her own and resents the fact he belongs to another woman, and sometimes has to phone home and she has to retreat to the bar by the hotel lobby when he does so. She wants a boyfriend she can meet whenever she wishes, to have a coffee, to discuss books and politics, to laugh along with. Her married lover seldom laughs, as his mind is not always completely there.

He had a reading the other night in a subterranean club near the Bowery and she was jealous because she knew the story he was reading from, accompanied by a melancholy Nick Cave and Warren Ellis soundtrack, the CD of which he had brought along and carefully timed to accompany his words, had been inspired by a woman whom he knew before her. She wondered whether one day he would write books about her. He did. Three novels and a handful of short stories, but by then they were no longer together because she had reluctantly called a halt to their relationship. She knew she was breaking his heart even though he agreed it was best in view of their age difference. Both were aware they had no possible future together.

She had arrived in New York a day late, having misplaced her passport the morning before while having a coffee and some pastry at a bar in Barcelona airport and missed her flight, until it was located and she was rescheduled to travel 24 hours later. She had called him in tears with news of the delay.

He was the first man she had properly slept with. Fucked. And quickly realised in his arms that she enjoyed the act of fucking. It was all she had expected and more.

Six months later both back in Europe, he came to visit her in Rome and they enjoyed an illicit weekend in a hotel a half hour away from the city, where they stood out as, he reckoned, the archetypal May to September couple among the few other guests, the older man with the younger girl. She drove him back to the airport and they both knew this was the last time they would see each other. It was for their own good, but it still hurt.

She would block him from her Facebook page and somehow disappeared altogether from the Net, despite her journalistic career taking off. She must have arranged it that way to fool the search machines, but then she had always been more fluent with technology than him, probably something to do with the generational gap.

She disappeared from his life like a character from a JG Ballard novel who ventures into the jungle in search of untold, enigmatic dreams and personal cravings and is obliterated from the surface of the planet.

She had wild curly hair, her breasts were small and ever so delicate to the touch of his fingers and his mouth, her dark pubic hair was untrimmed and a box of treasures and a light brown stain the shape of Sicily spread across her inner right thigh; she joked she was a fervent communist and she enjoyed wearing vintage clothes.

They made love in a ski resort in the Alps while a song by

Pink Floyd played on her computer while they coupled and he had an epiphany that she would be the last great love of his life right as he penetrated her for the first time and was overcome by the warmth of her body encircling him inside and outside. They made love in the medieval village of Calcatta, a half hour north of Rome, in London, in New York, Barcelona and a beach resort to its south and that final occasion by a lake in Italy close to the castle where George Clooney or some other celebrity had married.

He had always promised to take her to New Orleans and long wondered if it would have changed her mind.

And now she was a ghost, living only in his memory. More prosaically, she was probably now married with kids, partnered with somebody nearer her own age, no longer an avowed communist and freelancing for Italian newspapers and radio. But he wrote the books and stories about her, in which she appeared as in a hall of mirrors, none of them telling the actual truth about their relationship, skirting it, improvising around it, concealing facts, narrating what had happened and what might have happened. It was all he could do. It was all he knew how to do, turning the grief into words.

4. KATE CALLAGHAN

Her backside was a thing of beauty, and reminded him of Nicole Kidman's in *Eyes Wide Shut.* Pale and firm, standing between a thin waist and sturdy legs. She walked with long, manly strides and the way it moved, whether unveiled or closely espousing her form beneath pencil or billowing skirts, made it impossible for him to look away, turning his raging lust into something priapic.

She was also taller than him, an Amazonian princess with a head full of blond, corkscrew hair, her deluge of curls a small jungle through which he constantly craved to drag his fingers through. She had Irish antecedents and had read English at Cambridge and worked as an editor in publishing.

They were introduced to each other at a conference in the Midlands but had no professional excuses to keep in touch with each other, even more so as he had inadvertently given a smattering of bad reviews to several books she had acquired and published.

But he couldn't get her out of his mind.

He was a subscriber to a luxurious literary magazine devoted to erotica, which featured both short stories and fine art photography. In the current issue there was a black and white portfolio of images by an American photographer who was also know as a poet and the model, whose face was never seen in the photos, reminded him of Kate Callaghan, although at this stage he could only guess at the form of her body. He couldn't avoid masturbating over the images of this white, lanky and languorous geography of naked flesh sprawled over sofas and sand, her face always out of shot, but belonging to Kate in his imagination. He had a complicated relationship with pornography despite his own sensible public persona.

The feelings kept on stirring inside him, daily coming to the boil and he finally gave up and wrote her a letter, which he posted to her office, in which he casually confirmed how pleasant it had been to connect in Nottingham and maybe they could meet again for a drink or a bite one day to discuss the art of crime writing - the one thing they so far had in common. He ended the short letter, signing off "respectfully but lustfully". It caught her attention.

She was married, of course. But so was he.

Some years before, he had been one of the first critics to review JG Ballard's *Crash* in *New Scientist* magazine, of all places, where he was sometimes indulged and allowed to feature left of the field titles. He had described the novel as one of the first instances where sex and technology intermingled and his quote was picked up for years on the book's successive British paperback editions. At a private BAFTA preview of the Cronenberg screen adaptation, which Ballard attended, he was captivated by the face (and body) of the Canadian actress Kara Unger (before she changed her name to Deborah Kara Unger) and was also reminded of her when he met Kate. The sensual convergence between Kate and Nicole Kidman's arses manifested itself later, of course, once he had acquired carnal knowledge of the exquisite posterior in question.

They did meet for a drink; an evening of silences and hesitations and personal confessions in a West End pub. It was all he could do not to touch her knee or lean over for a kiss. She then had to travel home and catch her train at Charing Cross Station. He volunteered to drive her there although it was only a ten minute walk away. His car was parked in the large underground Chinatown car park. He was driving up the steep ramp to the car par's exit, his hand on the handbrake, the silence between them thunderous when, out of the blue, she laid her hand on his and he knew they would become lovers.

A week later they had made the necessary arrangements and driven to a hotel by Heathrow airport, where they hoped none of their common acquaintances were likely to see them book in for the day. He had brought along strawberries and a bottle of white wine.

Following their initial frantic couplings—it was all they had both expected, feverish desperate, rough, releasing days and months of frustration and desire—as they relaxed between the sweaty bed-sheets, he fed her the fruit while she sipped the wine. Later, in jest, he crushed the remaining strawberries and spread their mush across her lips, coloured her pale pink nipples with a brush of scarlet and, encouraged by her passive acceptance of his kink, painted her outer labia red. Now, she was truly an Amazon.

Another affair he would one day, after the bitter conclusion when she, in extremis, decided to remain with her husband, write stories about which she never forgave him for.

5. LOIS ELIZABETH HOUGH

He lived in the world of women.

Always had.

He was residing in Paris that year, and JG Ballard's *The Burning World* (which later became *The Drought*) was being serialised in *New Worlds* when he met her at a party for British expatriates. She hailed from Shepperton and had just arrived in Paris, and had found secretarial work at the OECD.

He was about to invite the friend she had arrived with, a curvy, small brunette with a winning smile, to dance when bloody Roland Thompson walked across his calculated trajectory and swooped the young woman away leaving him standing red-faced in front of her friend and obliged to invite her instead.

She might have been the wrong girl but they connected within minutes and later that night -or was it morning by then?—following a two hour walk by the banks of the Seine to his small, somewhat unhygienic apartment on Rue Saint Denis, they were making love in his bed. She was the first veritable girlfriend in his life or at any rate the first who was happy to sleep with him. She was sexually vastly more experienced than him; her move to Paris was because of a break-up with her previous boyfriend with whom she had lived with for over a year. She appeared to be happy enough with his initially clumsy lovemaking, and he never tempted the devil by questioning her further on the subject.

Her legs went on forever and she wore her hair long. She looked like all the pretty girls he saw in photos strolling down Carnaby Street back in London. He thought he was ugly and undeserving of her beauty and her body and never believed it would last.

They were both broke and outside of the bedroom had little in common. She didn't read books much and her taste in music was basic. The year before he had gone to the Olympia on the Boulevard des Capucines and seen the Beatles on the occasion of their first European tour. Seen was the word, as he could barely hear any of the music above the uninterrupted screaming of the audience. But he felt he was more of a Rolling Stones fan anyway. Their music was more primal and attuned to his senses.

It lasted three months and she grew bored of her job at the OECD and applied for new positions and was offered a transfer to Shanghai, which she readily accepted without even asking for his opinion.

A week before her departure, he slashed his wrists. Not very professionally as it happened, not having even bothered to research the proper way of doing so, and he barely lost any blood, although still today decades later if you look closely at his left wrist you can see the thin scarring lines in the right light.

They briefly corresponded.

On a holiday in Bali, she wrote to him about the still rumbling volcano hidden in the jungle she and her new boyfriend —a neurosurgeon from Montreal—had stumbled across. On another break, in the Phillipines she had taken photographs of herself holding the hand of yet another new lover, a swarthy Asian wearing mirrorshade sunglasses, on a beach still littered with WW2 defused artefacts and ammunition.

By then he had met Nicole, and he stopped answering Lois's occasional letters and postcards. Although he unfairly still yearned for those wondrous legs of hers, as Nicole was fairly short in stature. But he knew he was an imperfect man and understood his defects, always looking over his shoulders for better things to do, prettier women to watch or get involved with.

It was only years later when researching background for a story he was planning to write about the sex and fetish scene in Phuket in Thailand that he came across a photograph of a commemorative, massive basalt-stoned monument that had been erected by the entrance to Kamala Beach, listing the names of the victims of the recent tsunami, and one name jumped out at him: Lois Elizabeth Hough and her age.

She had drowned, alongside so many others, in the catastrophe.

That night he had vivid dreams of Lois a captive in her own private, drowned world, long legs akimbo, arms outstretched, mouth open wide, gasping for breath as her exploding lungs filled inexorably with sea water while the monstrous, mighty waves above crashed against the shore, dragging her helpless body along.

He woke up dripping with sweat.

For the first time in ages, he realised, his stomach tied up in painful knots, he was alone in the bed.

Without the presence, the body of a woman to calm his yearning heart.

'THE HARDOON LABYRINTH' BY J.G. BALLARD

It all began so innocuously.

I was returning from a trip to the rift valley of Lake Baikal where I had been despatched to report on a group of Brazilian artists and engineers who had contrived to mount an underwater performance of 'Sacred Pools', an opera by the late Vina Jackson, inspired by the works of JG Ballard. Lake Baikal covers a surface larger than Belgium, is notoriously deep and, at certain times of month, the freshwater is reportedly so saturated with oxygen that you can see almost up to 100m deep, hence its unusual choice as a venue.

The event was part of the annual Siberian Festival of the Oblique Arts, a celebration which had some years previously hosted the premiere of Dr Nathan's ill-fated attempt to combine a show of cloud sculpting by a French avant-garde troupe led by Louit Robert alongside a parallel manifestation of sound weaving by the unpredictable artist Arous Simone. Lake Baikal lies on a fault zone where the Earth's crust is slowly pulling apart, and a minor earthquake quickly upset all their preparations, sinking the project before it could be launched, financially ruining its creators, resulting in a double suicide involving the two revolutionary artists. At the subsequent inquest it transpired they had once been lovers, a decade or so previously, but had in the wake of the crumbling affair become bitter rivals. The collapse of their new collaboration and its implications for their hoped for reconciliation sounded the knell of their respective artistic ambitions and precipitated their death pact.

The opera, performed from a platform moored a hundred yards or so from the lake's southern shore, was something of a cacophony to my untrained ears. Music and voices underwater just feel distorted, even with the aid of state of the arts recording and broadcasting equipment . I was far from impressed even if I'm not much of an expert. I'm more of a rock'n roll sort of guy anyway. My views were shared by the majority of critics and I doubted it would ever be performed again following this fiasco. All that concerned me was that its supposed Ballardian influence was tenuous, if not unrecognisable, and that was all that mattered.

I was a Ballardologist.

I was paid by the Institute to travel the world and report back on the occult legacy of the great man's books. I just observed, read, listened, proffered the occasional opinion. I didn't know what happened to my reports; whether they were even read or just filed away in some vast repository of information or if any form of action was ever taken as a result. As long as I was paid (and I was; very well indeed).

Not that I needed the money: I'd never spent that much, unless it was on books and following my wife's decline into dementia, I had been left alone and hapless, with little purpose in life any longer. Every morning after I woke following a mostly insomniac night, the whole day lay ahead of me like an endless, arid desert I had to somehow cross and reach the other end of at sunset, a struggle between apathy and grief which had evolved into a sad routine, where the decision as to what to cook for dinner was the highlight of my day when I wasn't travelling for work.

I needed something to fill those empty hours and when I saw the advertisement in the back pages of The Bookseller trade magazine seeking out someone with a good knowledge of Ballard's works, I had thought why not and applied. I'd read most of his books and enjoyed, if not downright admired them, and I knew he had also lost a wife, albeit earlier than me and in very different circumstances. The commonality of grief made us companions in sorrow, I reckoned.

To my surprise, I had been offered the job.

Anything to mute the pain, the grief and the guilt was welcome if it kept my mind off the desolate path I was sadly stumbling across. It wasn't as if the work was arduous or I had much else to do.

I caught a mid-morning flight at Irkutsk airport which would take me to Moscow's Sheremetyevo where I would stay overnight at one of the many hotels that bordered the runways and would return home the following day. There's something immensely sad about airport hotels, I find. Sanctuaries worldwide set across the ley lines of flight, inhabited by temporary refugees stranded by missed connections or just waiting for transport to yet another maze of concrete runways, underground baggage conveyors and totally unnecessary shops selling the same international luxury brands regardless of where you were on the planet. If you closed your eyes while you navigated a maze of concourses, security checks and electronic display boards, you could as easily be in Bangkok, Dubai or JFK.

From my room window, if I pulled the curtains aside, I could just about catch the glimmer of Moscow's night lights in the distance. I couldn't understand any of the Russian programmes on the television set, and had no appetite for disparate versions of the news on CNN, BBC World or other imported channels. For a brief moment, I was overcome by a wave of loneliness. It was brought on by the overlapping combinations of identikit hotel rooms - I don't recall whether it was a Holiday Inn, a Radisson Marriott, a Hilton or whatever- and I stepped into my loafers, grabbed my jacket and headed for the corridor and the lifts, leaving the lights on in the room.

I was sitting on a high stool by the bar when she began a conversation.

She said her name was Emerelda Harding.

There was an aural fog of muted muzak that had me questioning what I thought I heard her say.

"Esmerelda? That's an unusual name. Were your parents fans of 'The Hunchback of Notre-Dame'?'

"It's Emerelda, without an S. I don't think either of them read a book in their whole life..."

I took a sip from my glass of tomato juice.

She looked exotic, her dark hair streaked with blue stripes, fell to her naked shoulders. She was wearing a shiny cocktail dress as if she had just walked straight in from a high society function. I was in jeans, sweatshirt and leather jacket.

My initial thought was that she might be a working girl on the prowl navigating her patch of airport hotel bars. But there was a glint of mischievousness in her green eyes that said otherwise. Whores display a deadness in their eyes, and she didn't fit that model. She also had a pronounced deep South America accent, New Orleans or thereabouts I thought, and could not be local. I reasoned that no classy American escort would be working the Moscow airport beat.

"Maybe they couldn't afford that extra ninth letter?" I joked.

"That's a more likely explanation," she said.

"Waiting for a morning flight?" I enquired.

She gestured for the barman, and when he slid over towards her on the other side of the counter, ordered herself a double espresso. She then slipped a hand into a pocket cleverly concealed in a fold of her dress at thigh level and pulled out a small business card.

She was from the Institute.

"How did you know I would be here tonight?" I asked her.

"We keep tabs on all our associates. Does that surprise you?"

It did.

"So this is business, not pleasure?"

She nodded.

"Something we have to discuss in private." she swallowed her coffee in a single gulp, grimaced and then suggested "Shall we go to the room?"

"How can I refuse?"

"Exactly."

Not an extra word was said between us as I followed her to the same floor where I was billeted, to a room that actually faced my own across the lengthy, gloomy corridor. Unsurprisingly it was a mirror image of mine.

She sat down on a corner of the bed and kicked her red-soled heels off.

"So what is this about?" I asked Emerelda Harding. "Couldn't it have waited until I was back in London?"

"I've enjoyed reading your reports," she said. So someone

72

was actually reading them. I felt a brief pang of satisfaction. "Something has come up and the powers that be felt you could be the best operative for the new job. And I was curious to see what you looked like. Not just your CV and a blurry photo on your file."

"I'm flattered."

She pointed to the mini-bar, which was lodged under the desk over which a flat screen TV was fixed to the wall. "I'm having a real drink now. You?"

"Just a fizzy drink if there are any in there. I'll take a look."

"So it's true. Says in your file you don't touch alcohol?"

It wasn't something I had ever included in my CV. Someone at the Institute had evidently researched me.

I stepped over to the small fridge. There was a line of tiny bottles of scotch, brandy and, of course, vodka and a single, orphaned, miniscule can of Coke. "There is. What's your poison, Emerelda?"

"I'll take the brandy," she said.

I handed her the small bottle, which she unscrewed and brought to her lips. She sighed as the warmth of the alcohol reached her throat. "You don't know what you're missing," she remarked.

I was trying to think of a possible witty repartee, but she spoke before I could.

"Have you heard of 'The Hardoon Labyrinth?" she asked me.

"Should I have?"

"It's a short story Ballard wrote in the mid 1950s. It was never published. No one truly knows why. The Estate considers it minor and unfinished and have never allowed it to be printed."

It now rang a bell with me.

Somehow a French publisher had somehow managed to make a copy of it, from the JGB papers held by the British Library, and included it in a new collected edition of the *Vermilion Sands* stories. But when the Estate had found out, they had gone nuclear and legal and forced the publisher in question to pulp every single copy, as the story's rights had not been specifically included in the publishing contract.

Emerelda explained that a few stray copies had escaped the fate of the print run and allegedly survived. They were now eagerly coveted by collectors .

"OK. So, what is the problem now?"

'The pages stored in the JGB papers at the British Library have been stolen."

"I'm not a detective," was my knee jerk response.

"We are aware of that, but it was thought your particular talents might come in handy. We are to team up to find where the manuscript might now be."

"Oh."

"Your daily fee will be doubled for the occasion."

"That's very generous of the Institute. But I wouldn't know where to begin. You seem to know a lot more than I do about the case."

"I do. We have a definite suspect. A rich collector."

"Good."

"There are not many Ballard memorabilia collectors. We knew of one on an island near Vancouver. But he has been discounted. Our technicians have monitored all his telephone communications for the past months and found nothing suspicious. He actually has a transcript of the manuscript pages of the story, which he obtained ages ago anyway, so it would have been perverse to have the actual pages stolen..."

"So the story is not completely lost," I interrupted Emerelda's account.

"The narrative isn't, but that's not the point. There is a subtext."

"I'm not sure I understand."

"We believe there is some sort of code embedded into the manuscript pages."

She made it sound as if the whole shebang was straight out of a Ballard story.

"Who is your suspect?"

"A reclusive and wealthy architect who lives in a gated estate in the South of France."

"Isaac Hardoon, you mean?"

"Yes; none other."

I was familiar with the name, had of course read much about him. His swimming pool designs were famous for their eccentricity and cost. He had devised increasingly outrageous and bizarre pools for celebrities, oligarchs and politicians worldwide. No photos of him allegedly existed.

"But if I recall, from a magazine profile I read, Isaac Hardoon was just a young child, barely born, when Ballard wrote the story, wasn't he? He couldn't have known about him."

"That's just the point. There is a dissonance here. The story is actually about an architect."

Curiouser and curiouser. But I was intrigued and willing to follow Emerelda down the rabbit hole. For twice my daily fee and expenses. We would catch the first available flight out of Moscow and head for France. Destination Montpellier airport with a connection at Paris Charles de Gaulle.

The flat wetlands of the Camargue, with faint clusters of pink herons dotted along their surface, stretched out below us as our flight approached its destination. Emerelda wasn't much of a travelling companion, dozing off into deep, uninterrupted sleep, within minutes of both our take-offs. Her way of recharging her batteries, I reckoned. I, on the other hand, had barely slept. Too many distractions: inhaling her perfume which I couldn't quite place, both floral and green, distant and aggressive, feeling the warmth of her body sitting to my right radiating in my direction, an unavoidable closeness, regularly declining the offer of further drinks from diligent air hostesses with frozen smiles, ever consulting the map on the small TV screen indicating where we were now flying over and somehow never quite confirming we were making much progress. Flying does not make me nervous; it just bores me and in the rush of catching our flights I had not had the time to pick up a book or two, and the in-flight magazines were useless, making me feel that I'd seen them on countless occasions previously even though they were the very latest issues, content repeated from month to month for captive travellers.

Emerelda had arranged for a car hire and after picking up our minimal luggage we took the road to the coast.

Hardoon's gated estate had been built just a few miles away from the Grande Motte resort, an architectural monstrosity once a forefront of brutalist fashion, but now looking more like an off-white concrete bunker, with its parade of identical balconies dotted along its facia like minimalist mouths carved into its blank geometric face.

We'd been booked by the Institute at the Heliopolis.

"What? A nudist resort?"

"Of course not," Emerelda informed me. 'Not that one, the Heliopolis you're thinking of is off an island near Hyères on the Côte d'Azur. This one is classier and you won't have to show your naughty bits."

Which came as a relief, although the brief prospect of witnessing her hidden parts might have been pleasant, and I was sure there would have been nothing naughty about them either. Since I had been alone, the prospect of sex was an ambiguous one. Its appeal constantly shadowed by a lifetime of grief and regrets.

Emerelda was, I realised, the first woman I had been this close to since the illness had taken my wife.

"Snap out of it!" she broke my reverie.

"What is your plan of action, then?"

"Pretty straightforward really: we break into the property and snoop around. Hardoon is at his house in the Galapagos right now."

"There must be security, though?"

"I assume so, but we'll be careful."

"I'm not sure that's quite what I signed up for."

"Didn't you read the small print?"

Once in my room, I drew the curtains. Outside, the sun was going down below the line of the horizon, the sky turning to copper. I went online and tried to find out as much as I could about Hardoon, his French estate and anything that might prove useful in the task ahead of us. I wasn't even sure why they needed me here, to be honest. There was little I could contribute, either in the way of smuggling our way onto Hardoon's property, or to seek out a few sheets of paper in a mansion that no doubt would present us with a sheer labyrinth of endless, vast rooms, nooks and crannies and, more likely, a sturdy safe - even if my companion in illegality had the wherewithal to force one open.

I initially assumed that as an architect of renown, Hardoon would have designed his Languedoc retreat himself and would have invited press and magazines to feature it in their glossy lifestyle pages, but there were no images of the place anywhere. Zilch.

The estate was the size of half a dozen soccer pitches and sprawled between a bank of low sand dunes and a mass of wetland ponds where the wildlife was under environmental protection. The only entrance was apparently reached through a coastal road whose initial access was guarded by a pillbox and a road barrier manned by security guards at all times.

I reported back to Emerelda.

"It would be useful to know the lay of the land before we make any attempt to break our way into the grounds," I remarked.

"I'd planned for that," she said.

We were on the balcony of her suite with a full view of the beach where parallel lines of deeply tanned bodies, most of them nude, lay immobile like chocolate soldiers, or oversized fish carcasses swept up by the waves and abandoned to their fate, occasionally twitching or turning over in eerie unison to perfect the ritual offering of their shocking intimacy to the roast of the fiery sun above.

Emerelda opened the parcel which had recently been delivered to her room by a hotel employee, after the front desk had advised her of its arrival. A small drone. Matte black. Spidery. Sleek.

"We'll fly this over the area. I'll connect its camera to my laptop. We can get an idea of the lay of the land."

"You certainly think of everything," I noted.

"Which is why I get paid the big bucks..." She smiled. She had changed into skinny jeans and a white T-shirt which looked moulded to her body. She wore no shoes in the room. Her feet were dainty. Her hair was wet and curling, fresh from a shower.

Someone once wrote that writing about music was akin to dancing about architecture. They were wrong on both counts. I loved music and couldn't live without it; music made life bearable. And as to architecture, well... The landscape below over which the drone floated was like a chessboard and literally danced in front of our eyes, a maze of swimming pools dotted across the perimeter of Hardoon's estate. The blue waters shimmered, wavelets radiating from end to end like folds of liquid silk.

"Why so many swimming pools?" I questioned.

I began trying to count them, managing to tick off nineteen before the drone, under Emerelda's guidance, abandoned them in the distance and was now hovering above the actual house at the far right end corner of the estate. Compared to the jewelled pools and the sheer vastness of the grounds surrounding it, it was rather modest. Italianate in style, steady white columns of, possibly, marble supporting a recessed porch, stucco walls, orange-tiled roof, a surprising helter skelter of styles, as if the whole building had been assembled from jigsaw pieces. It was so unlike anything from Hardoon's past catalogue, an afterthought after all his energy and creativity had been used up by the design of the myriad swimming pools, each one a different shape, a different mood.

Not all the pools were filled with water.

Some were empty, white tiles exposed to the sun. Others cobalt blue liquid.

Each one a cipher embedded into the landscape, a form of alien geography.

"Caldwell, were you counting how many there are?" she asked me. She must have spied the faint movement of my lips.

"Actually, I did. I made it nineteen... I think..."

"That makes sense," Emerelda remarked.

"I don't understand."

"How many novels did JG Ballard write?"

I dug into my memory, even began counting on my fingers, but she cut me short.

"Nineteen..." she explained.

"Are you sure." It felt more than I remembered.

"I'm counting both *The Atrocity Exhibition* and *Running Wild* as novels," Emerelda continued.

"That could be disputed," I interjected.

"Let's not be technical. Anyway, that's also the number of handwritten sheets of the stolen manuscript of 'The Hardoon Labyrinth'..."

"Makes it all sound like some crazy Dan Brown conspiracy. A bit far-fetched, no? Soon you'll be telling me the Knight Templars are involved or that Ballard wrote the story on segments of the Turin Shroud!"

"Who knows? At any rate, it bears further investigation."

I looked up at Emerelda. She was consumed by deep thoughts, alive to possibilities. On a mission. After guiding the drone back to our balcony, we retreated to the air-conditioned cool of her hotel room. Her wild hair was backlit, illuminated by the light rushing through the windows. She reminded me of Medusa. She was on fire. Amazonian. Fierce; her green eyes deep and intense, a Sargasso Sea of turmoil and excitement.

Damn it, she was beautiful, I realised.

"I'll make my way onto the grounds tonight," she said. "Just some reconnaissance. I'll go on my own."

"Are you certain?"

"Just to get an initial feel for the place. I need to take a closer look at the pools. Particularly the empty ones. Just in case they begin to fill them in the morning. I don't want to miss anything out. Something tells me they are a key to the whole affair."

"Your call."

We had supper together, Mostly seafood, which was delicious. I've always had a soft spot for oysters, and gorged myself on a two oyster course dinner: beginning with a dozen raw ones, followed by a further dozen grilled over an open fire, with a light cheese and garlic sauce. Emerelda went for the lobster. We both abstained from wine as she wanted to keep her mind clear for the task ahead and me because I was, more simply, tee-total.

"I'll see you at breakfast," she advised me as she headed back to her room, where she was planning to change into something more appropriate for her incursion onto the Hardoon estate.

That was the last I ever saw of Emerelda Harding.

She did not join me at breakfast in the Heliopolis dining room, and half a day went by without my hearing from her, which led me to go knocking on her door shortly after midday and get no response. Later, by mid-afternoon, I had a call from someone at the Institute enquiring about her whereabouts. I assumed she had stayed out late on her solo mission, was now resting and knocked at her door again. I then asked a housemaid who was packing up her trolley in the corridor to check on the room. We found it empty.

I experienced a difficult night. Maybe it was the fact that I was staying by the sea and in the wonderfully lazy environment of a holiday resort but I couldn't help being kept awake by a tsunami of memories of past times together by pools or shore with D, when I still had a life, when I was happy. Only to be stabbed by the recognition that we would never do so again. She and I would never return to Sitges or Amsterdam, the Maldives, Cancun, Puerta Plata, Bondi Beach, Sri Lanka, Phuket, the Stockholm Archipelago, cruise down foreign rivers or anywhere. I knew it was a form of PTSD, combining grief, guilt and all too many regrets that we hadn't done more together or that I had been a better husband to her. But being aware didn't fucking help in the slightest. By the following morning, I was exhausted by having slept so badly, so erratically that I somehow hadn't thought of Emerelda's absence further.

Another call from the Institute snapped me out of that particular slough of despond.

I was informed that Emeralda was dead and I should return to London forthwith. Arrangements were being made for me to supply a written statement to the police before I left but I was firmly reminded I was sworn to secrecy as to the reason for our presence on the Languedoc coast. I was to declare I was just a business acolyte of hers and that we had come to Heliopolis to scout locations for a documentary which the Institute was financing. The fact that we had stayed in different rooms precluded any thought of a possible romantic relationship.

Her body had been found by one of the gardeners tending the grounds.

She had drowned, I was told. Although her body, clad in a black nylon cat suit, was discovered towards the deep end of a drained swimming pool situated furthest from Hardoon's house.

It was later revealed, post-autopsy, that large amounts of seawater were found in her lungs, which made no sense but then nothing about the whole affair did. She was clutching sheets of paper in her left hand, but the ink and whatever had been written of them had long been erased by water and could not be retrieved.

Back in London I could not help but think of her pale, long body on a mortuary slab, the stainless steel apparatus of human butchery laid out close to her, being carved open from her throat downwards to her pubic bone. Even though I had never seen Emerelda naked, it was indelibly imprinted on my mind that her perfect mound would be smooth and in my terrible perversion that she would have a minuscule tattoo just above her hipbone displaying either a small gun or a number. Sig Sauer? 19?

I was shocked that I was having such awful thoughts about a dead woman, but I couldn't help myself.

A month or so later, there was a lengthy obituary online revealing that Hardoon had committed suicide. He had ventured from the Galapagos to the coast of Ecuador and embarked on an expedition into the jungle to, reportedly, seek out a local volcano for reasons unknown. After a lengthy trek with indigenous guides, he had reportedly slit his own throat once they had reached its initial slopes. He had left no letter of explanation and there was increasing speculation about his reasons: he was wealthy, famous, unattached and had no known financial problems, something of a recluse.

Tributes poured in, praising his contribution to modern architecture, his innovative genius and post-modern sense of design that according to some writers combined the brutalist and the art deco or was it the rococo? One commentator even alluded to the nineteen swimming pools on his French estate as a late-life aberration, a stain on his legacy .

I advised the Institute that I was resigning from my consultancy and there was no protest. I had just been a minor cog in their activities, I reckoned.

I sat at home, still thinking of my late wife, of Emerelda Harding, so many what ifs and the twisting road of life and the branches I had not explored, missed in my blindness.

I also thought a lot of all the other women I had once known, some only briefly, some platonically, some carnally, a kind of mental requiem for my troubled past. Until it all became something of a blur in my mind, bodies, faces, voices, scents, like a secret code I was unable to decipher, an unattainable formula that would provide me with peace. Somehow this perpetual jumble of emotions and images had become a shifting geometry of swimming pools, smiling mouths, limbs akimbo in oh so sweet surrender, as if the topography of Hardoon's nineteen mad pools was now impossibly interlinked with all my most intimate secrets.

In the night, the pools called out to me.

I woke up even more tired than when I had gone to bed, with subtle pain in all the places I never knew I had (thank you, Leonard Cohen). I lingered in bed, lacking any motivation to get up.

I was shaken from my torpor by the sound of the post falling to the floor by the door and the metal flap of the letter box against the wood. Just more books, I guessed.

When I eventually walked barefoot down the stairs and picked up the delivery, I noticed a large orange envelope amongst the Jiffy bags and junk mail paraphernalia. It was handwritten, and the calligraphy actually reminded me of Ballard's distinctive penmanship. I carried all the mail to the front room, sat myself down and opened the envelope.

There were nineteen pages. Each one numbered.

I shuddered. It was a copy of 'The Hardoon Labyrinth'.

I reached for my reading glasses and looked down at the opening page.

It all began so innocuously.

I was returning from a trip to the rift valley of Lake Baikal where I had been despatched to report on a group of Brazilian artists and engineers who had contrived to mount an underwater performance of 'Sacred Pools', an opera by the late Vina Jackson, inspired by the works of JG Ballard. Lake Baikal covers a surface larger than Belgium, is notoriously deep and, at certain times of month, the freshwater is reportedly so saturated with oxygen that you can see almost up to 100m deep, hence its unusual choice as a venue...

Nicholas Royle photograph

THE MJ/JGB LETTERS

1. Dear J.G. Ballard,

I revisited *Empire Of The Sun* the other day and was struck once again by those searing images of empty swimming pools stretched out under the coruscating sun of the wartime Shanghai of your youth. The way they carved a place in the catacombs of your mind while still a child and still echo to this day in everything you write and describe. I was then immediately reminded of all the other swimming pools dotted across the shores of your books and stories, in the *Vermilion Sands* tales and elsewhere, whose solitary ghosts have since become an evocative leitmotif like no other.

It somehow set me thinking back to the pools that have figured in my own life. Not that I can acknowledge as striking an influence. But then I pause and hark back to my younger years; as you did.

I grew up in a big city. Paris. Swimming was never a major concern. For several years, the family would travel back to London on the occasion of holidays. My parents hadn't yet opted to visit beaches or coastal resorts. This was long before mass tourism, or maybe they were just behind the times.

For two years in succession, we vacationed in the Alps, as the cold mountain air had been recommended by our doctor after I'd developed some shadow on my lungs. The health scare fortunately came to nothing and I retain powerful memories of cycling daily around the valleys, pretending in my mind that I was a 'coureur' in the Tour de France. The twisting roads and snow-covered mountain peaks surrounding us became the initial trigger for my first fictional story a year or so later when our teacher Monsieur Laurent suggested we not write a dry essay that week but instead exercise our imagination.

In that debut tale, I was snatched from my bike by a low-flying eagle and taken to its nest in the heights. The story was acclaimed best by the class and posted to the classroom wall. From that moment onwards, all I wanted to be in life was to be a writer, and no longer a cycling champion. A seminal moment; you could even argue that a bicycle and an eagle were thus my equivalents to your empty swimming pools!

I don't recall which of my father or mother, or both for once in agreement, decided when I was just eight years old that the time had come for me to learn to swim. I was despatched to a public swimming pool at the intersection of the Boulevard de Belleville and the Rue Ménilmontant, which was hidden away towards the end of long, gloomy courtyard.

I can still remember the stench of chlorine, the stuffy atmosphere of the place and the sadism of the instructor. At my second lesson I was still nervously hesitant to venture into the deep end and he got annoyed at my insistent reluctance and unceremoniously threw me in for disobeying his instructions. I must have swallowed half the damn pool in my struggle to keep my head above the surface while all the other kids laughed at me. To my parents' dismay and incomprehension I refused point blank to ever attend a third lesson.

Once we returned to London—again a city—we would often drive down to Southend on a Saturday, but the nearest we would get to the actual sea was walking down the promenade. The sea looked much too cold to swim in, anyway. As a consequence of all this, I didn't learn to actually swim until my late teens. To this day, I am still a pretty mediocre swimmer and my technique is clumsy at best as I never allow my mouth to ever move under water as I breaststroke, a small feat in its own right.

Growing older, I steadily grew an addiction to tropical climes and beaches but even though toes cautiously treading warm sand and the sometimes uneven seabed while the breeze flowing from the ocean is burnishing my tan became something of a drug of choice, I continued to prefer dipping into the resorts' swimming pools rather than the unpredictable waves and sometimes treacherous eddies and dips of the untamed waters. A feeling of safety.

I close my eyes and recall all those pools in Sri Lanka, St Lucia, the infinity one in Mauritius when, by our own fault, we travelled at the wrong time of year and the light of day ended much too early while we soaked in the infinity pool that looked out onto the calm ocean and the evenings went on forever. Not so much indelible images like in your stories, but each weighed with memories. Of the woman who was there with me.

But it's a swimming pool in Sitges, just an hour's drive south of Barcelona, in a hotel by the marina, that holds the more striking of those recollections. Shielded from the port by a low wall, overlooked by a multitude of balconies, lullabied by the sound of the wind drifting like a will o' the wisp around the masts of the yachts, small bells tinkling, marine smells lingering in the air and mingling with the odours of food from the parade of overpriced restaurants further down the promenade. Port Sitges.

The marina is wedged between two beaches, one a busy, sprawling family one, the other a narrower cove surrounded by rocks and a steep hill, which is clothes optional and at one end mostly populated by gay men, with often surprisingly-sized endowments and genital piercings. The hotel pool is like the magnetic pole situated at equal distance from both beaches, a psychogeographic ley line between familiarity and wildness, a place, a spatial architecture with secret, hidden meanings for those on the right wavelength. Of which I must be one.

The memory returns, sharply in focus. Standing, shamelessly, with my back to the pool's tiled circumference, two thirds of the way to the deep end, submerged up to my midriff. The sun is high in the sky. I am alone in the swimming pool. By the shallow end, D is dozing on her lounger, her book open and abandoned on her stomach, topless, her perfect breasts wet with perspiration. Dotted around the walls of the pool, at regular intervals, are small circular vents through which jets of compressed water shoot into the quiet, undisturbed waters, refreshing it, recirculating its contents. An endless cycle of regeneration.

My hand casually moves sideways to cover the vent, feeling the force of the jet struggling against my palm, blocking it, negating its powerful flow. Without thinking I tiptoe sideways and position my body so that the blast of the vent is now in alignment with my asshole. I slide my trunks down and pull my hand away. The rushing jet of compressed water bursts through, my sphincter its target. I take a deep breath, pull my

cheeks open and allow the powerful thrust of the submerged column of water to assault my opening, forcing its way into my bowels. I imagine this is like being raped would feel. By nature. I keep my features impassive as I relish the sensation; briefly recall a scabrous story by Chuck Pahlaniuk also set in a swimming pool where the character is not penetrated but has his guts sucked out of his body in similar circumstances. But this is safe; pleasurable even. My cock hardens. I come. My seed dissolves around me as it spreads its thin emission through the thousands of litres of water filling the pool, scattered, diluted, rendered harmless by the chlorine, wasted.

Later, reflecting on the improvised sex act I had instinctively allowed myself to indulge in I could only justify the profound wantonness of its unhygienic nature by comparing it to others or kids urinating whilst in the pool; surely, this was more harmless?

We were on a fortnight's holiday and I repeated the act several times again, whenever the swimming pool was empty, and even on a couple of occasions, when there were a few others busy completing athletic lengths on the far side, unaware of my disgusting activity.

Mr Ballard, this is my unapologetic confession.

Yours sincerely.

2. Dear Jim,

It was great spending a week with you and Claire at the Mystery Film Festival in Viareggio. What a marvellous hotel that was! Falling to pieces and reliant on old, decadent glories, but with a sweet 1930s charm and, sorry to say, no swimming pool to exercise our imaginations! At least the beach was situated just across the road once you had zigzagged through the incessant seafront traffic.

A damn pity, though, that the movies being shown, both in and out of the competition, were on the whole something of a disappointment. But wonderful for you to be given that Raymond Chandler Award, and for us guests to have been able to spend time with so many fascinating people.

Circumstances prevented us from interacting much with Nic Roeg and his wife, actress Theresa Russell, as he was on jury duty and too often shielded from us literary mortals. Some of his films have left an indelible mark on me. I could watch Don't Look Now and several others of his over and over and still get the shivers!

I'm uncertain whether it was a highlight or not when on the final, prize-giving evening, I was corralled into going on stage to accept the best actor award on behalf of Jeremy Irons for his part in Steven Soderbergh's Kafka as I was, apart from you, the only other Brit available (and you'd preceded me on the stage already). I can still hear the sound in my ears of the major collective sigh of disappointment.

From the audience as I walked out from the theatre's wing following the announcement of Irons' name, confirming once and for all I had neither his charisma or fame…

Ironically, after carting the trophy back to London and contacting the actor's management to try and organise a possible formal handing over of the award at somewhere like the National Film Theatre, they (or Jeremy) expressed total disinterest and all these decades later the physical award, a large, engraved silver sculpture, still sits gathering dust somewhere in my attic! Thus, my own obituary will probably mention I won three minor literary awards but also appropriated a film one…

Writing, as I am, of obits and death, did I ever tell you that for many years I was totally obsessed by your short story 'The Volcano Dances' (alongside 'The Mountain' by our mutual pal Mike Moorcock, which seemed to draw on similar, atavistic and seminal themes)?

Although properly Ballardian, the story resonates with me in curious ways that go so damn deep. Jungles, fate, immolation, death. I just don't know why. I've never travelled through tropical jungles or been attracted by their siren song, being more of a beach person, as I think you are too. It's been a long time since I've read the story last, but I know that the image of characters standing on the edge of a crater and being swayed by the seductive song of the earth's core crying out from below, connected with me in arcane ways.

Maybe because as a teenager Jules Verne's *Journey To The Centre Of The Earth* must have made a strong impression on me, ad did later a lesser-known novel by Catalan author Albert Sánchez Piñol *Pandora In The Congo*, in which some of the characters make a similar claustrophobic journey through the bowels of the planet.

I'll leave future critics or psychoanalysts to decipher the profound meaning of this fascination and will remain safely on the side-line! Does it annoy you when your own work is dissected in such a manner, autopsied to death by so-called experts and ascribed motivations you very likely had no clue about? You're no longer here to object but, if you were, I think you'd just smile wryly and elegantly keep your silence as the English gentleman you always were.

Under your influence, I once wrote a scene in an unpublished novel (a collaborative book which didn't turn out as we hoped) in which a man takes a woman he has ambivalent feelings about up to the cratered summit of a dead volcano in an unnamed foreign island and, after much hesitation, conspires to trip her and send her flying down into its maw. I later cannibalised this scene in another novel, but this time around he grabbed her arm at the last minute and she didn't die. I can envisage the thesis already: "Return to the primeval core; Instances of obsession in the works of Maxim Jakubowski"! At any rate, I won't be around to see it...

But I have had a thesis written about me, albeit in my guise as a translator… But that's another story altogether.

Wherever you are now, Jim, I hope your ghost is unable to look down on us and read all the rubbish these people who didn't even know you are writing about you.

I will stay in touch.

3. Dear Jimmy,

Cars. Ah, cars!

At the time you published *Crash* we were not terribly close yet; more social acquaintances with my smuggling the William Burroughs Olympia Press editions from Paris to you via Mike our only connection.

I had this weird gig reviewing new books on occasion for *New Scientist* magazine. The then editor was trying to expand his audience and for just a few months I was allowed to cover titles or subjects which normally they wouldn't have touched with a barge pole. I was the first critic to review an odd production that was playing in a small experimental theatre off the King's Road of *The Rocky Horror Show*, before it transferred to the West End and became a cult hit. This earned me some kudos. I had convinced the magazine that because of the monsters with echoes of Frankenstein, there was some sort of spurious link to science!

My next contribution was a review of Ian Hunter's rock 'n roll diaries; I still don't know how I sold that particular idea and linked it to the magazine's remit but I had vicariously enjoyed the book and its anecdotes and was a fan of Mott the Hoople's music. Naturally, I had my breath taken away by *Crash* and getting the review published was an easier sell. I came up with the notorious tagline of the novel being the first to intersect pornography with modern technology which the publishers quickly picked up on and used on later paperback editions and which was then quoted ad infinitum,

91

even though seldom attributed to me. I probably only described the book that way to justify submitting the review to *New Scientist*!

The curious thing was that, to this day, I have had little interest in cars. I only learned to drive in my late 20s, when offered my first company car. I see motor vehicles as a means to an end, to get from A to B when necessary. Neither am I a petrol head nor have I had any major accidents since I began to drive. Just a few scrapes, minor fender benders mostly when parking; nothing that has caused injuries to myself, passengers or others, or inflicted scars.

So why did the book affect me so much? Probably the fetishism and the fatalism, the way it offered sex a whole new dimension and normalised its abnormality.

Freaks like us, eh?

I was once given a blow job while driving down a motorway. Between Heathrow and Reading on the M4 on a drive to Exeter if I remember correctly. And it didn't cause me to crash! But unlike so many others I have never made love in a car. Or is that an American tradition only? Come to think of it, the most erotic experience I have ever had in a car was whilst driving out of an underground garage in London's Chinatown in my BMW and K affectionately touched my hand as I was holding the hand brake. Like a bolt of electricity racing through my body. That was the moment I knew we would become lovers and that my life would change overnight.

So, there you are. We do have something in common after all.

4. Message in a Bottle

Do you remember the time we travelled to Paris together? I'd been contacted by my acquaintances Stan and Sophie Barets who ran Temps Futurs, a small science fiction bookstore in the Latin Quarter. The premises were so exiguous it could barely host more than half a dozen customers at a time but was conveniently located, as just a few streets away from the hotel I would always use when visiting the French capital. They had managed to organise signing parties with most of the elite of not only French SF but also many visiting authors from overseas, but confessed to me that one of their greatest ambitions was to have you present. However, they had the impression, through your publishers or urban legend, that you were mysterious and unapproachable, a sort of 'hermit of

Shepperton', and not the convivial chap we all knew you were.

I passed on their invitation and a date was set. As it was you were already a frequent visitor to France, driving to the South most summers in search of sun and holidays, already developing a fascination for the quirks of mass tourism. It took very little to convince you and I agreed to tag along as your interpreter.

It was quite a coup for Stan and Sophie: the first public appearance in France of the great J.G. Ballard! The event put them on the map. Soon after they moved the bookstore to larger premises and even launched into book publishing themselves (introducing many of Mike Moorcock's titles and others to a French readership); in later days Stan even became the editor of the French edition of *Playboy* before his untimely death. We spent three days being effusively wined and dined by all and sundry. I still recall fervent discussions with various French editors and authors about the emerging punk music scene, with Robert Louit arguing that the Sex Pistols were the future of rock, and my insisting loudly that Eddie and the Hot Rods would instead survive the test of time. I was badly wrong as it happened, and ironically two years later, after changing editorial jobs actually became the Sex Pistols' official publisher, still half-famous today for commissioning *The Sid Vicious Family Album* and luring Moorcock into penning a novelisation of *The Great Rock 'N Roll Swindle* movie!

The memory remains fuzzy but I think you didn't return to London on the Eurostar with me, but moved on South to the Mediterranean where you were meeting up with Claire. No doubt in search of the haven of another beach.

Another commonality.

Even though we both prominently use beaches in our stories, I'm aware that the subterranean motivations that take us there originate from different places altogether. I've come to realise that for the past decade or so, at least, these sandy expanses have been invading my own stories and books in clandestine ways as I become more aware of my impending mortality. The correlation being that every beach I've visited reminds me of happier times that I will no longer be able to recapture. Of places and women. Of sensations. They do not serve as metaphors. For me, they are not signposts for the atomic age or the near future, but tombstones alongst the road of my past.

Happier times.

Digging in the wet, muddy sand for baby crabs or other buried crustaceans off the coast of Brittany. Lusting after girls on the Mediterranean during that summer of sheer madness on my first solo holiday; although right now I am unable to even recollect the name of any of them any longer: desire is so transient!

A cold beach in Northern Spain where Michel and I clumsily tried to seduce two German tourists, an epic failure but four decades later I managed to shoehorn the sorry tale in a story about the Beatles' 'Eleanor Rigby', which was that summer all over the radio just a week or so before the release of the *Revolver* album.

A wild beach in the Languedoc where a bunch of writers were taken on a furlough from the conference we were attending nearby and found ourselves skinny dipping. No doubt a historical first, but discretion remains the order of the day as to who was actually present in a state of total undress...

The golden sands and remote dunes of Cap d'Agde, where we spent our first nude summer, eventually succumbing to peer pressure and disrobing fully. I still have that polaroid, D. My guilty, beautiful secret. A beach in Patagonia, which mermaids visit. Fictional, of course; I don't even know if they have proper beaches in Patagonia and was too lazy to research. A terminal beach of sorts where my principal character willingly surrenders his manhood to the siren song of a warrior princess who will then triumphantly swim away with her necklace of severed male parts circling her throat.

All those beaches are now a blur. A confused landscape of coasts, islands, and sand, waves and sounds; a film score full of epiphanies and heartbreak.

An isolated atoll in the Maldives where, at low tide, we could wade a mile knee high in the water to a nearby uninhabited island from our hut on stilts. The narrow beach was full of third world detritus, plastic bottles, seaweed, broken branches, a sandy Sargasso of screeching birds, the interior of the small island a thicket of trees and malodorous smells. I understand it has since been cleaned up and built on and is yet another, tropical all-inclusive resort.

The Rendez-Vous in St Lucia. Trelawny in Jamaica. Sri Lanka. Phuket. Sitges. Cancun. Bay Cove in Barbados. Puerta Aventuras, where you could go swimming with dolphins and gaze at the lazy manatees. Corfu. A whole palette of plush resorts in the Dominican Republic. The Hedonism adults only resort near Montego Bay where I had won an all expenses paid holiday in a writing competition, the theme of which was 'sand and sun', ironically enough.

I was halfway through penning my ten volume pseudonymous erotic saga in response to *Fifty Shades* and had to stick to a 2,000 words a day typing regime whilst there because of pressing deadlines. It was such a sordid place that whenever I was stuck, attempting yet again to add some originality to an obligatory sex scene, all I had to do was leave our bungalow and wander down the beach and voyeuristically watch all the brazen sexual activities on full display all over: not just beach, but pools, jacuzzi, shore, pergolas... For once there was no need for any time-consuming research!

Just names.

Just beaches.

Only *Vermilion Sands* is missing!

Sometimes, during sleepless nights, I wake up thinking that had you ever visited those beaches instead of me, you might have written different things. But then so would I... Other eyes, other memories.

Are there beaches in paradise, purgatory or even hell? Or wherever you are now.

It's mid-morning on a grey, bleak day in London as I sit reminiscing and writing to you, just a half hour from Shepperton. This is my final report from the deep end, Jimmy.

Your erstwhile friend, Maxim.

CRUISING FOR A KILLING

In Nuku-Hiva, in the Marquesas Islands of French Polynesia, the local population normally stands at around 2,660 people (and hundreds of sharks in the neighbouring waters that you are requested to not feed, at any rate voluntarily) only for a weekly or so cruise boat to swell the numbers by several hundred souls, disembarking at the jetty from the tender boats, to the sound of a local haka and the beating of tribal drums, a task that keeps one per cent of the island's inhabitants in work and dressed for the occasion in traditional attire which they probably hate with a vengeance.

We'd been at sea for nine days since the boat had left Acapulco, and the prospect of solid land had us queuing like lemmings on the stairs leading down to Deck Three where we could embark on the smaller crafts that would take us ashore as the cruise boat was anchored some five hundred yards away from the island which lacked suitable mooring facilities large enough to accommodate it, unlike our previous ports of call.

I'd travelled on the *M/V Magellan* once before, as a guest lecturer giving talks on Agatha Christie, Miss Marple, Hercule Poirot, Chandler and Philip Marlowe, Sherlock Holmes and Inspector Morse, in my capacity as a crime writer. I'd suggested to the cruise company a series of talks on the British speculative fiction New Wave: Moorcock, Ballard, Aldiss, Bayley et al, but they had found the prospect too adventurous for their audience, which I understood. It was a nice, easy gig, even if on that occasion the audience had mostly consisted of retirees and geriatrics ticking off their bucket list by cruising down the Amazon. Two elderly passengers had in fact died on that cruise, of natural causes, which I was told by someone on the medical team, was not uncommon and that the boat's facilities had suitable space enough to fit up to half a dozen dead bodies in between ports. It was a not uncommon feature of cruising that the large companies who owned the giant boats did not advertise in their glossy brochures designed to attract the older generations and the grey pound (or dollar or euro).

As a result of this earlier cruise I'd become familiar with the vessel's systems. On embarkation, every passenger was handed a personal cruise card, the size of a credit card, which he or she would use to bill all purchases and bar bills to his account. In addition, this card functioned as an I.D. document of sorts and was scanned every time the passenger would go ashore at a port and again when he returned on board, thus informing the ship's main computer if anyone had been left behind. It seemed pretty fool-proof and well thought out until I discovered by accident that there was a serious loophole in the system.

So as not to have to carry the card in my shorts pockets all the time, I had made a habit of storing it when not needed inside the top drawer of the desk in my cabin only to find, one morning, it had seemingly disappeared. I'd assumed that I had lost it somewhere during the previous day when I had been carrying it to go ashore and promptly made my way to the reception desk to have the cruise card cancelled and prevent any other passenger who might have found it of using it and charging drinks or worse to my account. The Ukrainian blonde manning the desk was all smiles and agreed to do so with immediate effect and then printed out a new card for me, no further questions asked, after checking her screen and confirming that no extraneous charges had been posted to my account. Maybe it had fallen out of my pocket shortly after I remembered using it last following my excursion into Recife, laden as I was with both my rucksack and a shopping bag of various souvenirs? My worries put to rest, I placed the new card inside the drawer only to notice that the old, presumed missing cruise card, was in fact still there and had just slipped into a corner and had jammed itself flat against the partition of the drawer and was invisible to the naked eye from a certain perspective. I breathed a sigh of relief but decided not to advise the reception desk and appearing something of a myopic imbecile. The old, cancelled cruise card would make a good bookmark, I reckoned, and a sober reminder to myself to be more careful in future.

Crime writers being what they are, it gave me the germ of an idea and a couple of evenings later, noticing Daria, the Ukrainian girl from the reception desk off-duty around one the bars I fell into conversation with her and we spent a pleasant couple of hours in discussion during which time I asked her a handful of questions about the way the boat and its systems worked, mentally storing away the information.

"So, your missing cruise card, it did not reappear?" she asked.

"No," I lied.

"Is OK then," she continued. "But no one can use it to make you pay for drinks you not have," she laughed.

"It was so easy to cancel," I mentioned, sipping slowly from my tall glass of Prosecco. Daria was drinking vodka. "We have good security system," she added. "All I do is cancel the way the card charges; all rest I leave unchanged."

A bell rang in my head and, on the occasion of our next shore visit, in Rio, I tested the system by using my original cruise card when I disembarked, half expecting the white-uniformed cadet who was manning the exit desk by the gangway and was scanning the passengers' I.D. to stop me and point out my card was somehow no longer valid. He didn't. Returning from the city a few hours later, I deliberately used the new card to check my theory and, again, it passed muster, confirming that the personal details electronically inscribed into both the invalid and the valid cruise cards did not clash and were in fact strictly identical.

Maybe one day I'd be able to use this fact in a story, I thought.

And soon I would, but not the way I'd previously expected.

I'd met Ophelia at a book signing. We authors don't have 'groupies' the way rock musicians are rumoured to liberally accumulate. I suppose there's nothing glamorous about typing at a keyboard in silence for hours on end and emerging, blurry-eyed, into the world every year or so with a new volume, and if we're lucky, to whore it as best we can in sparsely populated public libraries, far flung literary conferences and enjoy the attentions of at least a couple of reviewers who have actually read the book, and ventured beyond the press release. So, being confronted at the end of the signing by a reasonably pretty young woman, with long dark hair, who had visibly read a few of my previous novels and wanted to know when I would be writing again about Dominick and Summer, my feisty, ever-quarrelling society amateur sleuths and signalled, with a broad smile flying across her scarlet lips, how annoyed she had been that I had seemingly killed Dominick off with a heart attack at the outset of what I hoped would be the final book to feature the characters. I'd been sick and tired of them and would happily have despatched both Dominick and Summer, preferably torn to pieces by rampaging zombies or annihilated in a worldwide pandemic, had my literary agent and editor not counselled otherwise, and suggested I allow some ambiguity in the finale. Was Dominick really dead, or was it all a ruse to be explained in a future instalment, no doubt in a bid to mystify their nemesis Jackson Vine? I was beginning to think I had been maybe a bit rash as the new book I was promoting, a stand alone with a brand new investigator (who also happened to be a killer) had so far only sold half what my books usually did, and the crowd at this particular signing had been sparse and uncommunicative. Even Ophelia hadn't actually bought the book at the store but had brought her copy along, no doubt acquired online at a discount that meant I would only be getting a reduced royalty on the sale.

I tried to defend my reasons for what she considered to be Dominick's murder but she stood her ground, arguing I did not have the right to get rid of a much-loved (by her) character. She was getting on my nerves, but then again she was rather pretty, in an English Rose sort of way that often touched me inside, so I began flirting with her, for lack of anything else to do right then.

"Actually, you know, there's a lot of me in Dominick," I revealed, with a sly smile.

"I thought there must be; gut feeling, I guess" Ophelia said. "That also made me angry, you see."

"Really?"

"Whenever I was reading about him, I'd often turn to the dust jacket and see your photo and thought he must look a bit like you..." she said.

Dominick only drank Coca Cola while I preferred wine. He always dressed with a strong sense of fashion which allowed me to pad the narrative with lots of name of labels and superfluous descriptions of clothes (although Summer allowed me even more licence on that front) while I always wore black Farah trousers (I alternated between half a dozen similar pairs) and loafers. Dominic was extremely rich and I was nothing of the sorts. But Ophelia was quite welcome to think of me that way.

The bookshop assistant picked up the small pile of a dozen or so books I had signed without being asked, to ensure they remained for some time in the store and were not returned to the publisher's warehouse. A trick of the trade you get taught with your very first book. A writing game of survival! The shop was growing quiet, just late evening punters browsing unenthusiastically or seeking shelter from the thin drizzle of a London autumn evening outside. I looked up at Ophelia. Her eyes locked with mine. How again had I signed the book for her, I tried to recall? Had it been a standard indifferent dedication, or had I been more effusive?

"Well, that's me done," I said, as I rose from the chair and stepped away from the table. "Care for a drink and we can chat a bit more?"

"I'd love that," Ophelia said.

Affairs are often like flash floods. They begin with a rush of lust, a torrent of words and you momentarily believe they will drain everything in sight and mind in their wake, only to fade out under the pressure of time and life until all that is left is the steam rising from the street gutters, the shadow of what once was, the X-ray of perceived love. Or maybe I was just too demanding, unable to compromise, too misanthropic or selfish.

At first, I found Ophelia amusing, affectionate, sexy, cheeky and devoted. Until one morning, her obligatory idiosyncratic traits began, one slow inch at a time, to irritate me, annoy me, irk me and I began to wish we had never met. I have no wish to go all porno here and relate the exquisite, intimate details of our lengthy tryst; I'm not that sort of writer. Neither do I have any intention of going into all the psychological ramifications involving the two of us and why, at the end of the day, I came to the unhappy conclusion that we were totally unsuitable for each other.

She'd come down from Scarborough via a minor redbrick university where she'd, of course, done media studies. She had no extant family, few friends -maybe those she'd once had had seen through her early and avoided her presence—and, damn it, she was possessive. By sleeping with me she curiously felt she owned a part of me, wanting to know all about the book ideas I had, hoping to influence me, become my muse so to speak, seeking some form of minor glory from her carnal relationship with me, when all I sought was the carnal, no more than that, and flinched at the idea of anything serious. I was too much of a loner and basically selfish for that.

I was about to call an end to what we had, for whatever it was worth, but something inside me intuited that Ophelia was just not the sort of girl who would take the enforced break-up well. There was a dark side to her that I perceived, the potential for destruction. Self-destruction, possibly, or as a worst possible scenario my own. Stalker? Avenger? I knew she would not react well.

So, I dithered, continued sleeping with her, saw her weekly, resisted any suggestion she move in with me. She was in the final months of writing her thesis (on the male gaze in indie movies), and lived on a small inheritance from her parents who'd died some five years earlier in car accident in Lanzarote.

We were in bed, sheets humid with the sweat of our exertions, the silence now weighing heavily on both of us, the sounds reaching us through the half open window from the road at night fading as the traffic whittled down to a crawl.

"What are you thinking of?" she asked me.

A typical, inopportune Ophelia question. I was thinking

of nothing, blissfully oblivious to the whole world, still coming down from my earlier orgasm, calmly floating in that ineffable region between pleasure and oblivion.

"Nothing."

"Surely, you must be thinking of something, no? You're a creative sort of guy. I can't believe you can just switch off on demand."

"I can. It's a way of recharging my batteries, I suppose. What about you?"

"What? Thinking?"

"Yes."

"Well, you know our birthdays are coming up?"

We'd discovered at an early point in our relationship that our birthdays were coincidentally just a few days apart, even though I was a clear ten years older.

"So they are..."

"We should do something. Together. Go away, say, not letting any of our acquaintances know. A magical mystery journey somewhere."

"Hmm..."

"Wouldn't it be a great idea?" We'd once gone to Brighton for a few days and, on another occasion, Ophelia had accompanied me to a festival in Bristol, where she had annoyed me intensely by never leaving my side, seemingly attempting to bask in the glory of telling the world she was fucking an actual published writer. Had I not said: she also had ambitions to write but so far was all talk and no typing.

I nodded. I was no longer thinking of nothing. An idea had taken root. Knowing Ophelia would never go quietly, I had hit on a scenario that might prove fool proof.

A few days later, thoughts ordered, plan mentally moving from a fragmented jigsaw to reality.

"Have you ever been on a cruise?"

"Wow... For our birthdays, did you mean?'

"Yes."

"That would be just amazing."

"As you know I'm struggling a little with the looming deadline for the next book and I remembered what Larry Block once told me. He's often mentioned that he goes on cruises to get away from it all and be able to concentrate on writing and finds it incredibly productive."

He'd actually written that it was 'like being on a writer's retreat but without the distraction of all the other writers'. In this case. Ophelia would be the main distraction but her presence there would have both pros and cons.

"Where to?"

"French Polynesia and New Zealand."

"Amazing." It was an expression she liberally over-used and that often set me on edge.

"Tahiti, Bora Bora, both the New Zealand islands. We'd fly out to Acapulco to catch the boat and fly back from Wellington at the end of it."

"Amazing," Ophelia said again and I winced. "Do you think that in New Zealand we could visit *The Lord of the Rings* set. It's supposed to be fantastic?"

"I don't see why not."

The sail into Tahiti had proven a massive disappointment. I had memories of Paul Gauguin, topless natives, palm trees, Robert Louis Stevenson and all sorts of exotic vistas, but for over an hour and half we had navigated our way through a landscape of container docks, larger than any I'd ever seen, which, weather apart, could have fitted into any old Northern European bleak immensity of derelict industrial areas straight from a 1950s espionage thriller. Fortunately Papeete itself was an improvement, if a touch tawdry. We visited the Municipal Market where I bought Ophelia a necklace of black keisho pearls which I bargained down and felt quietly triumphant about for only to later see the same on another stall at yet a cheaper price. But she looked nice wearing it, even more so when we made love for the last time in our cabin by the light of a moon flickering like a will o'the wisp in the Marquesas Islands night.

I'd done my research and planned the deed for our next stop on the smaller island of Nuku-Hiva, which we would have to reach by tender as the dock was not geared for a large cruise vessel.

I'd made it a habit of carrying both our cruise cards in my shirt pocket, which Ophelia didn't mind as all our drinks and other expenses on the boat were charged to my account. Both were swiped by the officer in charge as we stepped onto the smaller vessel that would take us ashore. I also had a third cruise card, in my own name, in my shorts pocket, which I had obtained the previous day at the reception desk by having reported I might have mislaid my original one. I found a pretext to ask Ophelia to carry her own cruise card with her after we disembarked from the tender, by accidentally dropping it to the ground as we purchased a couple of soft drinks from a quayside vendor. But the one I gave her was, by sleight of hand, my spare one and her card remained safely in my pocket.

We hadn't booked an official excursion and had agreed to make our way through the small island on our own. I knew from earlier Googling in London all there was to know about Nuku-Hiva, possibly more than any local guide might know. Research is always a writer's best friend.

I had two options at my disposal.

Having made it a fair way across the island, we'd reached a small cove where, according to my information, the sharks congregated. There wasn't even a warning sign about their presence, as the spot was so secluded even few locals, let alone visiting tourists ever came this far. Sadly, there was only one around, visible in the distance and totally uninterested in our presence, racing through the far waters, ignoring us.

He looked rather large, though and Ophelia squirmed as she noticed him. Right there and then, I realised that I was not a violent man and was unable to begin struggling with Ophelia and throwing her in the water anyway. For all I knew, she might have been a rather good swimmer and able to escape quickly enough and there was no way I was about to summon the fortitude to hold her under as the shark approached. So plan one was a wash out.

Which left the crater of the dead volcano.

It was a hell of a climb and we were both sweating like hogs by the time we reached the top of the path leading to it.

Ophelia was complaining non-stop about the heat, tiredness and the mosquitoes which appeared to have a definite appetite for Boots Insect Repellent but I had managed to convince her to complete the trek as the views and the photos she would be able to take would truly be phenomenal, or in her own words, amazing.

Finally, we emerged from the twisting, narrow path.

We were literally in the clouds. Beneath us, the canopy of trees was like a second ocean, rivalling the principal one in the distance with its infinite variations of green and brown. The stillness in the air was like a thick cloak of pregnant silence. The black dust leading to the jagged crater crunched under our feet, topping the jagged edge that separated us from the void. I went first and peered down. It felt as if the slope winded down for miles into a foggy form of darkness. For a brief moment, it was like standing aeons back in time to a day when creation was still in its infancy, forming, shifting, literally alive. I drew my breath. A few steps behind me, Ophelia was taking photos of the jungle we'd left behind on her digital camera, sweeping it along as she took selfie after selfie or a panoramic video of the mighty landscapes surrounding us.

"It's truly unbelievable," she exclaimed.

"It is. Well worth the effort, eh?"

I suggested she move to the ledge and I take a photo of her, with the crater in the background. She hesitated a brief moment then agreed, putting a brave face on her rising vertigo.

She stood, a fixed smile on her face, looking back at me.

"I'm sorry," I said, and dropping the camera to the ground I rushed towards her. She first looked surprised, then questioning, then fear spread across her pale features as I made rough contact with her shoulders and pushed her back.

It lasted barely a second, but for what felt like an eternity she swayed on the spot, losing her balance, realising what was happening and finally toppled over backwards and her body began its fast, inexorable descent down the slopes of the crater. She remained silent all the way, until her white cotton shirt faded from view and I caught my breath again.

There were a lot of different things I could have said,

attempted to explain why I was doing this, why it made me unhappy but that I had no choice. That I had genuinely loved her but... But... But...

But real life is not like a story. Time passes faster, and you are nowhere as articulate as you can be on the printed page or the computer screen.

I picked up the small camera I had dropped, pulled out the memory card, broke it clumsily into a few pieces and threw both the camera and its remains down the wide crater to follow in Ophelia's trail.

I did hope she hadn't suffered long.

I hurriedly returned to the quay to catch the final tender back to the boat and made it just in time, as the climb up the volcano had taken so much longer than I had hoped or expected. Stepping onto the deck, I gave my cruise card to swipe, then shouted out that I forgotten my baseball cap on the bench of the tender and ran back to the embarkation to retrieve it. It was late in the day and the crew were too busy processing the returning crowd of passengers to take note of the fact that I had one of my cruise cards scanned a second time. Ophelia's absence from the boat would not create an alarm.

Job done.

I was now free.

I would play the same trick upon leaving the boat at the end of the cruise before being driven to the airport. According to all the computer records, Ophelia would duly have departed the Magellan on arrival in Wellington, as she had returned to the vessel in Nuku-Hiva.

Trust a crime writer to commit a perfect crime. Would I get away with it? Only time would tell, I reckoned, and that might be another story altogether.

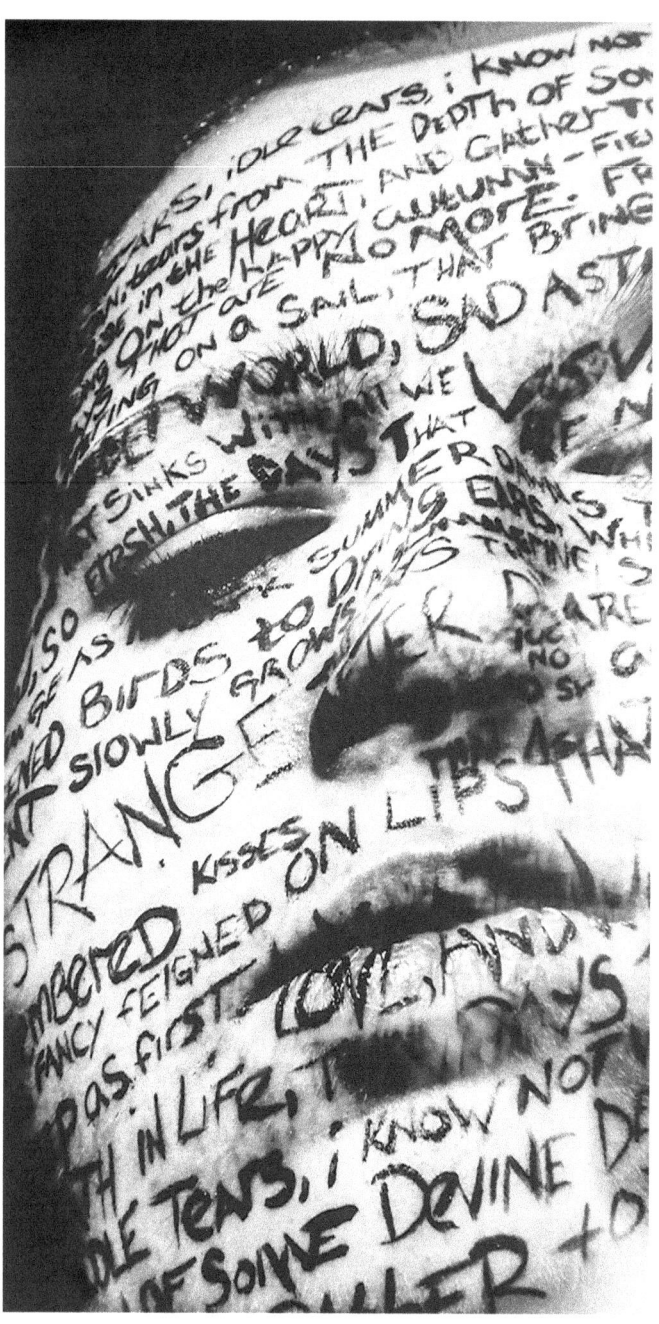

WHAT HAPPENS AFTER THE END

> "For to kill is the great law set by nature in the heart of existence! There is nothing more beautiful and honourable than killing!"
> Guy de Maupassant, 'Le Horla"; used by Cornell Woolrich as an epigraph to *The Bride Wore Black*.

He had come to the city to escape his past. He had committed a crime and attracted retribution. Although not from the authorities. What he had done was inconsequential in their eyes; others might have managed to get away with it, but he hadn't. A contract had been put out on him and death was coming. He was resigned to the idea.

The name of the city was equally unimportant. It wasn't Paris where he had spent many years until it had become a cemetery of broken love affairs. Nor was it New York, where he might have found it easier to hide amongst the multitudes of boroughs, skyscrapers and desolate tenements and the milling crowds the Big Apple attracted from all over the world: loners, refugees, romantics and outlaws. Or London or New Orleans, two more cities he knew well and could have navigated with ease and where he could have concealed his presence with a modicum of ease, lived in relative anonymity. And, for him, San Francisco was emotionally just out of the question, a place celebrated by the movies but which he had never quite connected with in the same way as most others despite its many celebrated charms.

He'd managed almost 18 months on his own. Feeling as if he was living on borrowed time, unable to enjoy what he knew would be his final days of freedom, ever on the look out for signs that he had been located, unable to plan for more than a few days ahead, acting all along as if everything and anything was just temporary. He could not find in himself to any longer attempt to read a book, in the knowledge he might never know how it ended; or begin watching a TV series, with the final episode shielded by future clouds possibly never to be seen.

He had never lived that way before. He had always been a man who made plans, lists of things to do and systematically ticked them off. There had always been a future ahead of him: a new movie to see, a vacation in an exotic place to look forward to, a meal in a familiar restaurant where he would inevitably mostly order the same items on the menu he had enjoyed before. It was like a strange sensation of running in place.

He did not have to work. He still had enough money from the job that had gone wrong and had turned him into a target. Days rolled by; some ever so slowly, dragging along, thoughts lazing through his head and never quite achieving fruition; others raced by until darkness came and he realised he had actually done, accomplished nothing.

It was a simple diner on a street corner, straight out of an Edward Hopper painting. He was sitting on a high stool by the zinc counter and had ordered a burger and a glass of cold home made lemonade. He was down to his last handful of fries, his mind in neutral, his eyes focused on a squabbling middle-aged couple in a booth at the far end whose arguments he could barely hear although the simmering anger that hung between them was betrayed by their body language. He enjoyed observing people, casually building up stories about them in his imagination. When they finally turned silent and began to concentrate on the plates of food on their table, he noticed that someone was now sitting on the stool to his right. It was a woman. Her perfume was quietly fragrant but elusive. She was blonde, her hair cascading down to her shoulders, its silky ends draping themselves across the top of her brown leather jacket. He initially thought she looked a bit like Taylor Swift. She was perusing the laminated menu.

He had always been partial to blondes. His first blonde had broken his teenage heart and caused him to clumsily lacerate his wrists in a bid to keep her; it hadn't worked but he still had the small scar that reminded him of Lois Elizabeth. The next blonde he had married; her name was Laura. The final blonde had been called Katherine and their affair had lasted six months and broken up his marriage.

The young woman turned towards him. Maybe not Taylor

Swift, he thought; there was something steely and glacial about her that actually made her appear even more alluring, polished like a diamond. Deadly, beautiful.

"How's the burger?" she asked. She had a foreign accent he couldn't quite pinpoint.

"Decent, actually"

She had grey eyes and the moment he looked into them he both fell in lust and realised instantly she was his angel of death. The time had finally come. It wasn't at all what he had expected, but he rather enjoyed the thought that this was the woman who would kill him.

She smiled at him. He smiled back.

Words unsaid, particulars kept in the dark: by the following morning, he was dead. Knife? Gun? Poison? Pills? Overdose? Fall from a great height? Strangled?

It mattered not in the order of things.

Cornelia had always enjoyed a curious relationship with hotel rooms.

She had lived in many, although never for extended periods. She had killed in a fair few. She had slept with men, strangers she had picked up on a whim when she had been in need of sex or men she had lured to a pre-booked room or agreed to follow to theirs with anything but sex in her own mind, just the job in hand. So hotel rooms had become associated in her mind with lust or death, an uneasy combination. But, as a result, she never visited the same hotel twice. Maybe, at the back of her mind it was a fear the front desk computer reservation system might allocate her the same room in which she had once either fucked or killed. There was also the fact that when she was the one making a booking, she always registered under a different name, and never bothered to keep a record of which she had used or where. Always settling by cash, of course. She had called herself Carlotta Valdes on several occasions; also Judy, Madeleine, Julie or even Julia Russell.

But those days were, she reckoned, long behind her now. Her book collection had been growing exponentially and just over a year ago, she had taken a long lease on an apartment downtown in another city, if only to have a proper place to shelve her rare volumes, away from the storage facilities in the suburbs where she had only limited access to her treasures, tidily boxed up in darkness like abandoned children.

Cornelia had always been a voracious reader, from early childhood all the way through to university, although could only afford cheap or used paperbacks then, and relied on public libraries to sate her appetite for the written word and the way those words somehow transformed into stories that transported her both into the mind of others but to other worlds too. She hadn't completed her course and had dropped out after her first year, her patience growing thin with the unemotional dissecting focus her professors and tutors applied to books and, which to Cornelia, felt like a wholesale betrayal of the purpose of literature. She had been brought up by distant relatives following the passing of her parents in a car crash when she was only in her teens and felt no compulsion to stay in touch with the distant second-hand family she had been offloaded onto. She had first moved to New York, and rather than fall into the traps and McJobs of the low gig economy, she had almost accidentally become a stripper. All those men kept on telling her that she had a body to die for, and that she moved with sultry sexiness, and wasn't she always coming across 'wanted' ads for exotic dancers displayed outside the clubs that littered the North area of Times Square or in the free papers available on most street corners? She loved music anyway, and it turned out she moved like a natural. So what difference did it make whether she performed dressed or undressed? She saw the stripping as just a craft, and it was much more appealing and relaxing than dancing for tickets in dance halls, or escorting. Cornelia had never been overly emotional, unless she had surrendered heart and soul to a story in a book where the characters felt so much more real than most of the people she chanced across in civilian life. Acquaintances often told her there was a coldness that surrounded her like a halo, which neither pleased nor displeased her. It was just the way she was.

A fairly rare title by an author she collected assiduously

had surfaced on the market; an early proof with substantial handwritten annotations by the writer which had been carried through to the final published version and substantially changed the original plot and the fate of some of the fictional characters involved. This not only made any copy of the advance reading proof valuable, but the changes visibly made in the author's hand had created a unique artefact.

The book was priced well beyond her means but she had asked the dealer for a fortnight's grace so she could raise the money; the antiquarian seller had agreed as she had been a reliable customer in the past.

Cornelia had pondered doing some escorting but quickly calculated the cost of the book would even then prove out of reach. There was a regular customer at the strip club who, she knew, had taken a fancy to her and repeatedly offered her drinks following her final set of the evening. He had often drunkenly boasted of possible criminal connections. It was through Vito Bonaparte she made contact with the fixer. Her looks counted in her favour, as no one would ever become suspicious of her, and she quickly demonstrated she was a pretty good markswoman, having been given lessons in handling a firearm by her father and shown surprising aptitude. She was given a photograph and an address. The rest was up to her. The hit she contracted for was twice worth the book she coveted. She did not hesitate. She justified killing a man to herself by arguing inside her mind that someone else would carry out the killing had she turned the opportunity down and that the target was a dead man walking anyway, so why not benefit from the job?

Afterwards, she felt no guilt and experienced no nightmares. The money was good enough to appease her relaxed conscience.

A few weeks later, she was offered another hit in a different city. One more rare book for her collection. She was professional and careful not to get caught on security cameras, leave fingerprints or allow anyone to witness her presence on the scene or the vicinity of the crime. Other assignments followed. The death broker always supplied the weapon, which she disposed of afterwards although she decided after the first handful of hits that she should not restrict herself to guns only, and began using other methods so that she didn't adhere to a specific trademark.

Her collection of rare and antiquarian books kept on growing. In the wake of bodies left in her wake.

Cornelia had been a killer for hire for three years when, for the first time, she thought she recognised one of her victims; he was crossing Houston by the corner of Wooster Street. She was walking north in the direction of Union Square where she had intended to browse through the new arrivals at Barnes & Noble. She remembered him well. She had slit his throat, taking him by surprise while he was pouring drinks, pre-bedroom, in the vast penthouse space he occupied on the Upper East Side just a few blocks away from the Met. It had just been a year ago as she clearly remembered that it was the day the translation of the final Elena Ferrante novel in the Naples Quartet had been published and she had picked up a copy earlier in the day and had to rush back to the Airbnb she had been staying in for the duration of the assignment to change into evening wear to meet up with her hit. He was a man with coarse manners who advertised his lack of taste with pride, enormous Rolex watch, gold medallions and an expensive tailor-made three-piece suit which no honest citizen would wear in so shiny a fabric. Cornelia tried to recall his name but her memory was unreliable. Once a kill had been completed she had a habit of drawing a line on the job once and for all. She stood still, watching the man hail a yellow cab, thinking it must surely be someone else who looked like him, but he was wearing the same stupid silk necktie, with a pattern of gold embroidered hawks against a night black background. Surely, this could not be the same man? Or an identical twin? The hit had been successful and there was no coming back from that.

There was nothing else to do but dismiss the idea and forget. Just some eerie coincidence, she decided. Or maybe she should get her eyes tested?

Two days later, sitting in Washington Square Park and sipping a tepid coffee while reading a book in which a ballet dancer in Montreal was turned into a wooden puppet, Cornelia's attention was drawn to a nearby nanny chiding her curly-haired, cherubic-like ward who was throwing pieces of the cupcake he had just crumbled towards the marauding squirrels. As she looked across the path, a woman in loose dungarees and outsized sunglasses jogged by, pulling a dog on a leash behind her. Cornelia had never been animal friendly and could not for the life of her distinguish between canine breeds, but she recalled having had to lock the animal into the bathroom on the night she had killed Sicilia Ann. Who right now was running past her bench, her sneakers hitting the ground in metronomic rhythm.

Sicilia Ann. It was the only hit she had undertaken against someone she had previously known in her personal life. Sicilia Ann had worked as a stripper in the same club where Cornelia was contracted that particular summer, was the queen of the pole and had incredible breasts which were the envy of all the other dancers. Cornelia's chest was more modest, not that it had ever bothered her. Sicilia Ann had once worked as a microbiologist and, when dancing, billed herself as Doctor Ann. She was always dragging her fellow performers along to obscure street food eateries where she was always familiar with the cooks. Cornelia never wanted to know why someone was designated as a hit, but assumed Sicilia Ann had stumbled into some involvement with illegal drugs and was now having to pay the price for theft or betrayal of some sort. When she had received the large manila envelope with details of the assignment, it hadn't initially clicked until she had torn it open and glanced at the familiar face in the photograph; she had never been aware of her erstwhile colleague's family name and the fact she was of Italian descent.

It had been one of her easiest kills, with little need for subterfuge; just a drunken night out with a friend. Cornelia had wanted the death to be painless, and had simply twice injected Sicilia June with an air bubble directly into her veins, cutting off the blood supply to the brain. She had read about the process online.

And there she was rushing out of Washington Square Park, on the corner of Waverly Place, crossing past the boutique hotel that had once hosted Bob Dylan and many other cult figures, with her dog in tow. There was no doubt it was the same person; Cornelia clearly recognised the distinctive striped black and grey leotard she was wearing. Along with the familiar pink colouring of Sicilia June's pigtail ends. She rubbed her eyes, uncomprehending. This made no sense. She had even attended the young woman's funeral.

Her mind was fuzzy. In normal circumstances, she would have quickly stood up and followed the unlikely jogger, but she wasn't thinking clearly right now, her faculties blunted by the shock appearance of someone she clearly knew she had killed. Who shouldn't have been there. No way.

Cornelia wondered whether this was a message. Either her mind or the world out there was giving her a hint that she should put an end to her killings. It wasn't as if she needed the cash right now. She had all she wanted and enough set aside for rainy days or new books and she had never taken any particular pleasure in undertaking the hits, getting kicks from it; it had just been a job. One she did well and tool pride in, but no more. Not like an addiction she couldn't shake.

She looked down at her feet and caught sight of a brown squirrel negligently ambling along the narrow path, making its way to the patch of grass behind where she was sitting on the wooden bench.

Wrong animal, she wryly remarked to herself. She was not being drawn into a remake of *Alice in Wonderland*, and following it, or the jogger who looked like Sicilia Ann, down some existential rabbit hole in the ground. She was staying put. She took a final sip of her coffee. It was now cold. Dismissed the jumble of thoughts and emotions running around her brain like a turbulent tide, and attempted to go back to the book she was reading. The lines on the pages blurred and she couldn't recall which character was the wife and which was the mistress. She had never been a major fan of psychological domestic thrillers anyway.

Cornelia rose from the bench, dropping the half-read paperback to he ground and abandoning it. She was determined to clear her mind.

"I am sane," she remarked to herself as she stepped away from the bench and took off in the direction of Greenwich Avenue, "it's all an illusion, a form of dizziness, maybe a virus that I've caught which is distorting my perception. I am not in a film or a book, because that is where these sort of things happen. This is real life."

She sighed.

Back at her apartment, she enjoyed a leisurely bath, her body submerged in the warm water, its surface a landscape of fragrant bubbles, while Bruce Springsteen's 'Born to Run' played on the hi-fi and she hummed along to 'She's The One' she had put on repeat, her attention hypnotised by its insistent piano riff. Finally, the blanket of shimmering rainbow bubbles slowly faded away and she watched the contours of her body, the way her legs stretched away, long, shapely, her best asset she knew. As she shifted her position, her nipples came up for air, dripping bath water, their distinct shade of pink and light brown a familiar sight. They had always been coloured slightly differently, and, when she was younger, she had briefly thought of herself as a freak: the girl with different coloured nipples, but then one day she had come across photographs of the singer David Bowie, and noted how his eyes came in distinctly different shades, and she had accepted her oddity, even taken it to heart as a proof of her individuality. Her gaze wandered further down to her delta. She kept herself shaven; it was something of a professional obligation for the job as an ultimately nude dancer. Initially she had felt something like a plucked chicken, being bare down there but had long since become accustomed to the smoothness of her mound, and the way it divided cleanly, her labia peering with restrained discretion down its centre. Between her sex and her navel, slightly off to the left she displayed a tiny tattoo. An image of a small gun in black ink she had treated herself to on the occasion of her fifth kill. It was silly, she knew, but it made a strong impression on her punters and even more so on the rare instances when she allowed herself to take a man to bed for sex.

Stepping out of the bath, she towelled herself dry and slipped on a white oversized tee-shirt, then tiptoed to the main room of the apartment where all three walls were heavy with packed bookshelves. Remembering the puzzling sighting of her first kill a few days earlier, she walked over to the shelf where she kept her signed advance proofs, meaning to take a peek at the Le Carré *Night Manager* rarity she had managed to purchase thanks to that initial kill of the mob-related guy. It wasn't in its usual place. For the next hour, she kept on browsing through every single shelf in the room and was unable to find it. Cornelia was extremely organised. Considering her double life, she had to be, and was inordinately proud of the excellence of planning and her attention to detail. She had never misplaced a book before. Maybe she'd scour the shelves tomorrow again when her mind was less preoccupied by the recent improbable appearances of those disturbing ghosts from her past as a hit woman?

She tried to clear her mind of the troubling vision of June Ann jogging with her dog in Washington Square Park. Tried to recall which book she had acquired with the resulting fee that had rewarded that kill. It came to her: a dust-jacketed copy of Cornell Woolrich's sixth novel *Manhattan Love Song*, the final book in his Scott Fitzgeraldian phase before he turned to pulp and noir. She had actually never got round to reading it, always meaning to do so next and, anyway the cover was in a fragile state, as few copies had survived the weight of years past since its publication, which made it a coveted rarity wrapped in its transparent plastic book protector sleeve.

Again, she failed to locate it, despite a forensic search of her collection.

After a whole afternoon of frantic searching, Cornelia gave up in despair. Again, it made no sense: her apartment had not been broken in that she could see, and why the coincidence of those two particular books linked to the impossible reappearances of her two victims?

She was doing two shifts at one of the clubs she was currently working at that evening. She quickly packed her gear: the diminutive outfits she wore at the onset of each dance, her make-up bag, her music tapes. She slammed the door behind her and checked twice she had properly locked the apartment up.

Every time Cornelia felt she had succeeded in blocking the memories of the sightings of her two phantom victims and her mind attained some form of peace, her focus returned to the disappearance of the two matching books from her collection. Appearances and disappearances.

The strip club operators were always critical of the music she chose to dance to. They would have preferred her to select more famous, familiar hits but Cornelia had idiosyncratic tastes, veering towards the obscure and her movements were always in perfect synchronisation to the music she had brought along, whether tunes by Aldous Harding, Leonard Cohen, Sharon Van Etten or The National. Not for her the bump and grind obligations of 'We Are the Champions' or 'Hey, Big Spender'.

"They're a bit gloomy, aren't they?' they said.

But once the music played she was at one with it, and the way her body moved in harmony with its melody and rhythm, how she orchestrated the unpeeling ritual of her clothes until she stood swaying totally bare in the spotlight on the elevated stage, paler than pale in the sheer glare of both the lighting and the eyes of the men who lusted for her was a thing of absolute beauty. Revealing, obscene and triumphant in the knowledge that every man in the room was captivated by the sight of her enigmatic smile, the gentle curves of her breasts and ass and the sexual heart at the crux of her body, the cunt of a hundred lustful attentions.

She was now fully naked, winding down her movements to the final chords of 'Candy's Room' when a man stood up from the shadows of the sparse audience and threw a banknote towards the stage. His face briefly traversed the beam of the spotlight and she recognised her last kill. It was without doubt the man she had made contact with at the Franconia Diner and later despatched. It had been a curious evening. He had greeted her as if he already knew who she was and was resigned to it. Accepting. He had never struggled, almost offered himself up to her, not even going through the pretence of trying to seduce her to justify her readily following him back to the hotel room she had booked for the occasion.

The music faded away. The lights went off. Cornelia left the stage, with a final look at the audience, anonymous faces scattered in the dimness that came in the aftermath of every dance. She sought out the face of the man who had stood up to tip her, noticing in passing that it was unusually a hundred dollar bill which she held crumpled in her fist as she stepped down and made her way to the backstage area where she could dress again. He was no more to be seen. Had it even been the same man?

"Did you see the guy in the audience who stood up to throw me a bill at the end of my set?" she asked Teresa, who served at the bar and had a fuller view of the small auditorium.

"The customers all look the same to me," Teresa answered.

Cornelia went straight home. She slept badly that night. First she dreamed, then she remembered every person she had killed. By morning, the bed-sheets were damp with her sweat.

Over the following weeks, she came across further random sightings of past victims.

At Chelsea Pier, a fleeting vision of the couple whose car she had sabotaged. On the down escalator at the Union Square Regal as she journeyed up on the opposite side, a middle-aged man with a pony tail, wearing a three piece suit and scuffed shoes; he had struggled and almost got the better of her and it taken several days for the scratches he had inflicted on her back to fade away. On the same day, crossing Broadway after the movie, she had to step back toward the pavement when a car raced around a corner and almost took her out; she caught a glimpse of the driver: it was a guy she had been forced to sleep with before she could get the opportunity to dispose of him; he had been rough and unpleasantly verbal and she had taken extra pleasure in discharging the whole barrel of the Sig Sauer straight into his heart. On the subway, briefly noting a familiar face on the platform as her Sixth Avenue Line train pulled out; a guy she had avoided the imposition of sleeping with, having managed to slip a pill into his drink and knocking him out before smothering him with a pillow while he dozed; she had a clear memory of that evening, having departed the hotel room with a swoop on its complimentary toiletries, having taken a shine to their fragrance, which she had been using ever since.

And the books kept on mysteriously disappearing from her shelves. Cornelia could now predict in advance which would have faded away into oblivion as she returned to the apartment following yet another sighting, equating titles with particular hits she had been involved in. One of the books she mourned most was an advance reading proof of J.G. Ballard's *The Atrocity Exhibition* in the US edition that was later pulped. It had cost her an arm and a leg. She began to despair.

There was no sense or reason to it. She felt as if she was living in a bad pulp story, but then even those have an ending of sorts. She wondered how hers would end.

The one thing she was certain about was that it wasn't guilt that was causing this disarray to her life. Cornelia did not believe in guilt. Just in books, sex and death.

She stopped working. Phoned the clubs she had been dancing in and advised them she was taking a break from the trade.

She felt adrift and forlorn, mourning her lost books and increasingly troubled by these regular apparitions of unlikely ghosts.

Unable to find sleep or peace, she finally reached her decision. She had always been proud of her lack of emotions and it was with a certain detachment that she went about her business.

She visited her bank and ordered a bankers draft by debit of her account, which could not be directly traced back to her. Then she walked down Canal Street and acquired a suitable burner phone from one of the many stalls selling rip off brand copies and all types of paraphernalia, and also managed to get hold of a small electronic scrambling device that would change her voice and make it unrecognisable to any listener.

The next day, using the phone, she called the fixer who normally provided her with jobs and made the necessary arrangements. They had actually never met in person and he was quite unaware of what she looked like; all their previous contacts had been over the phone and arranged through intermediaries. All he knew of her was her voice.

As instructed, Cornelia deposited the folder with her photograph and the bankers draft in a left luggage locker in Grand Central. He would have it picked up the following day, once he had checked the locker was not under any observation. She reckoned it would take a week or so before he managed to contract the job out, and whoever took on the job completed their research.

She returned to her Village apartment and waited.

There were so many books Cornelia owned she hadn't read. Maybe she would have time to complete a few before her killer came. And listen one final time to her favourite music by Counting Crows, Grant Lee Buffalo, Townes Van Zandt and others, wondering where it had all gone wrong.

She had requested the hit be fast and painless.

She didn't even lock her front door.

THE COAST OF NOSTALGIA
A Medical and Historical Jigsaw

THE TRUTH AND NOTHING BUT THE TRUTH

In times of reflection he often thinks of himself as a character in a story. Because he has spent such a large proportion of his life involved with books and movies. It has become the way he looks at life. He imagines what soundtrack might be playing at crucial moments. He wonders who might be the writer of the story. JG Ballard, John Irving, Marc Behm, Cornell Woolrich, Sara Gran, F. Scott Fitzgerald, Drieu la Rochelle, Emily St John Mandel, Boris Vian, André Pieyre de Mandiargues, James M. Cain, Pauline Réage? The list is endless. The tale is a melancholy one, but it is also erotic, mechanical, dotted with strange imagery, criminal, fantastical but because he is the only one who knows the truth at the heart of the story, its surface is also a clever hall of mirrors concealing the many failures in his actions and character he has no wish to advertise openly. He knows that after he is gone, no one is ever likely to write his biography or would be capable of sorting between the truth and the imagined, the bad things he has done, the countless fault lines and lies he has left in his path. Would it unimaginatively be called 'The Story of a Nobody' despite his occasional accomplishments? Or 'A Wasted Life'? Or even 'The Man Who Never Knew'? Let the author decide, he reckons, as he won't be around to argue. He has reached that stage in life when the first thing he looks for when he opens the pages of his daily newspaper is the obituary section. More and more there are names of people he has known personally, or that he has lived alongside like a familiar presence throughout his years. And if the names are unknown to him, he focuses immediately on their date of birth to see if they are younger or older than he now is. The way things are going he fears he might become the last man standing. Which is a lonely place to be.

AARANDALE DREAMS

She sits on the edge of the bed looking ahead. Her eyes are two-thirds closed and she is immobile. Her mind is broken. Memories and reality just blur together. She is not always aware of where she is. Her day is punctuated by the activities the nurses try and remind her of: shower, washing teeth, dressing, breakfast (bran flakes and raisins in milk), the vast desert of hours ticked off until lunch when she has to be fed by a carer, sitting in the armchair or the common room gazing at the darkness of the TV screen, the radio is left on playing popular classical music like a smooth caress, time passes by and then it's supper. In all those hours, she has barely said more than a few words, random sounds in the variety of languages she once knew, but never connected or making sense, the frustration seizing her, sometimes lashing out in anger. In moments of semi-lucidity, she asks to go home or enquires about both her father and mother who have been dead for over thirty years, but then her mind quickly wanders away from the ever-elusive thought and she reverts to apathy and quietness. Doctors visit and make notes. Plants her relatives brought wither and die. Somewhere in the terrifying depths of her brain, she is still there but she cannot be reached. She hugs visitors out of instinct, seemingly unsure as to who is who. In a way, she is dead but still alive physically. Once upon a time, she loved to lounge by swimming pools. Her past, now locked away, was an anthology of swimming pools. A communal one in Cap d'Agde, in the South of France, where she first saw her teenage daughter gallivanting topless in the water with her girlfriends and realising that she had now become middle-aged; the kidney-shaped pool at the resort in Phuket where the slope to the deep end was perilously abrupt; the circular pool at Hedonism in Jamaica where so many drunk vacationers swam naked and played somewhat obscenely; the Lego-like geometrical swimming pool at Club Palm Bay in Sri Lanka where the local birds had appropriated a small section and had to be shooed away by attendants, where the square blue tiled mosaic shimmered in the sun like an impressionist painting, her husband reading nearby on his deck chair and smiling enigmatically at her as he always did, a man who always kept his emotions private, his tan darkening by the hour. She sits on the edge of the bed, waiting for a nurse to come and fetch her or a visitor to visit, uncomprehending, her past life drifting inside her head, disconnected, like floating blobs in a lava lamp. As a young girl, she recalls, she once lived in Ukraine. But, most of all, she remembers all the swimming pools.

THE CEREMONIAL SODOMY OF VLADIMIR VLADIMIROVICH PUTIN CONSIDERED AS A WORK OF ART

Putin was launched on the downhill slope, strapped into a dentist's chair. Cornelia Jackson was holding the starter's gun and wore Jackie Kennedy's notorious pink pillbox hat. For her, this was just another job. Had she been asked, she would have dressed as a mermaid or any kind of femme fatale, no questions asked. Just two months earlier, the same shadowy employers had recruited her to play a naked crash test dummy in an experimental 16mm film filmed at Shepperton Studios. The compacted metal grey BMW 316i over which she had been draped was held in place by a complicated arrangement of pulleys and chains, and at the intersection where it had supposedly collided into a yellow Triumph, another model she had not come across before, whose name was Emerelda, was positioned with her limbs akimbo pretending to give a blow-job to the gear shift knob. She was allowed to be fully clothed, but Cornelia felt that even in her state of calculated undress, she was the more dignified of the two. The job had paid well so that was all that mattered to her. Putin was in a rear admiral's dress uniform, festooned with medals in a celebration of the colours of the rainbow. The signal was given and Cornelia depressed her finger on the trigger. The dentist's chair took flight down the steep slope. Putin had previously been gagged so any screams of terror were muted as the contraption and its prisoner steadily began their exponential acceleration. Her task accomplished, Cornelia looked up at the nearby screen

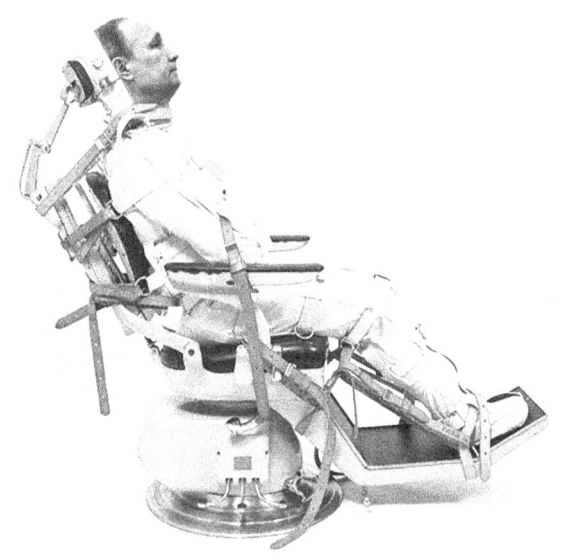

where Putin's journey was being recorded and broadcast live. There was no commentary and the silent movie unwinding had a strong sense of disconnect. There was a sharp angle in the road halfway down its descent and somehow, even though now at full speed, the dentist's chair and its cargo elegantly swerved round without crashing and continued its assigned course. A director in some remote location switched to a camera sited at the bottom of the hill and, on the screen, the chair and its captive dictator were seen rushing towards the finishing line. His face was red, his eyes bulging in sheer terror. Now visibly under the control of some unseen operator, the chair slid to a halt before it reached the buffers which had been installed at the bottom of the hill. A couple of orderlies stepped towards it and methodically unstrapped Putin, who now stood, unsteady, in his military uniform which had been tailored to fit as a straightjacket. For a brief moment, the whole scene froze until, instructions probably filtering into their ear-pieces, the burly orderlies stripped Putin down, shoved him onto his knees and hands and proceeded to vigorously mount him in turn, thrusting savagely into his rear to the sound of a Shostakovitch symphony, their lubricated king-size cocks working away at his pale arse like technological pistons of fate and retribution. After a while, Cornelia looked away. She knew this would not end well and had no appetite for butchery.

THE UKRAINE VORTEX

They had Ukraine in common. His mother's parents had been immigrants. Possibly because of pogroms, they had fled the city of Odessa shortly after the turn of the 20th century and travelled to England where they had settled and started a family. His mother had been their youngest child. He barely remembers his grandparents as they both passed away before he was five, and his only memories are triggered by fading black and white and sepia photographs in which they are seen holding him, a chubby unattractive baby, in their arms with a look of incomprehension in their eyes. His mother never spoke Ukrainian, only English. Half a continent away, D was born in Tadjikistan, of a Polish father who had survived the Spanish Civil War and a White Russian mother of noble descent who would also decades later succumb to dementia; they had been evacuated to the Russian Middle-East as a result of the ravages of World War II, but left it behind when she was only three and moved to the Donbas region of Ukraine where she initially grew up on a farm, as both her parents were agricultural engineers. Many years after they had met and become a couple, and after their own children had flown the nest, they talked about travelling to Ukraine together but never did get around to do so; he read books about Odessa, enjoyed the Cossack stories of Isaac Babel and held a deep fascination for all these seemingly fabled and remote places without which he would not have existed. They finally booked a river cruise, which would taken them from Odessa to Kyiv but then Covid struck and it was cancelled. He would never see Odessa's Jewish Quarter; not that he had ever felt particularly Jewish, let alone visited a synagogue; although he was circumcised. Bye bye Ukraine.

128

ANNA X IS DIVORCING

The woman who calls herself Montana, after a book he had written, sits on a Sunday morning by the pool of her compound outside Monrovia in Liberia. The Atlantic sea lies beyond a fence. She swam in it earlier but is now lounging by the pool and relaxing, emailing men she knows. Her NGO mission here has just three weeks more to run and she will then return to Sweden, where she will sit down with her husband and discuss the *modus operandi* of their mutually agreed divorce and how to break the news to their two teenage daughters. Anna X is 47 and she knows the clock is ticking on her hopes of a second life. Returning to the UK after a two decades in Stockholm, she knows she will need a job which will enable her to maintain a reasonable standard of living, pay for her dance classes and expensive lingerie as well as finance her daughters visiting her on a regular basis and having a room of their own wherever she settles down in the country she was born. For years she had fought her inner cravings, trying to make sense of the curious way in which the labyrinths of BDSM attracted her and her husband had proven amenable to her sexual quirks, even agreeing to visit swinger clubs together on a couple of occasions, although neither had partaken fully and proven to be more voyeurs of other bodies openly taking their pleasure and merely gone down on each other albeit in public, but it had not been enough to feed the appetite inside. Through the Internet, she had established a dynamic with a Master in the UK and willingly submitted to him, and following months of mutual hesitation actually visited him and gifted herself to him. It had felt liberating, both mentally and sexually, but he had later called the relationship off for a variety of reasons. Nonetheless, she had stuck to her plan of divorcing, even though there was no one now to go to. Change of country and job, change of life. This, she explains to Maxim J in a detailed email. He has become her confidant by default. She sits by the pool, soaking in the weekend sun, trying to read a book he had recommended to her or is it one of his pseudonymous ones? She is not a great reader, but enjoys noting down sentences or witticisms that strike a chord with her, and which she later uses as captions for the revealing but teasing photos she takes of herself and posts on a fetish site (which is how she and Maxim J had met). She dozes off and the book slips out her grasp and falls into the deep end of the swimming pool. Soaked by the water, it swells in size and soon sinks to the bottom.

SOU

She was born Annarita in Naples. She never liked her name and had people, friends, schoolmates and acquaintances call her Anita instead. Once she began selling her photographs to music magazines, she took a professional *nom de plume* and published her work as Soukizy. Intimates knew her as Sou. She contacted him out of the blue, through a common friend, when she asked if she could highlight a paragraph from one of his novels on her blog, where she jotted down thoughts, poems and words that had made an impression on her, alongside her early work as a photographer, evocative black and white images of bleak urban landscapes where high rise buildings and railway tracks blurred into grey skies and pictures of musicians at play she had taken at clubs and concerts. Encouraged by their

affinities, she sent him nude photographs she had self-taken. Not particularly explicit, a hint of nipple there, a convenient shadow across her pubes there, vast expanses of a pale back or shoulders. Some of the photos revealed a man's hand lingering across her skin. A boyfriend she no longer was with, she confessed, hinting at undercurrents he could only guess at. They had casually known each other for fifteen years and, by coincidence, made contact again following a long break in correspondence when both their circumstances changed. She had by now moved to Milan and was struggling to make ends meet as a freelance photographer and journalist mainly working for a leading local jazz magazine. He was not a lover of jazz and out of curiosity listened to much of the music and musicians she recommended but found they did not move his soul at all. It should maybe have proven a warning. But then he remembered that JG Ballard was not a great lover of music, and he shouldn't judge others by his own, sometimes quirky, musical tastes. She was fed up with Italy and he jokingly suggested she should move to London, or New York where the opportunities might be better. She had established a friendship with the American musician Bill Frisell on the occasions of his frequent gigs across Italy. During a Zoom chat, she mentioned Frisell was playing a big US festival in Knoxville, Tennessee, a couple of months later. She could get official accreditation but her magazine was unwilling to finance the travel and living expenses. 'I'll take you', he offered. Suggesting they could visit New Orleans together, as it was relatively close geographically-speaking, by European standards, and maybe even add New York to the journey. 'Would you?'" she asked. Of course, he would. He booked the flights and hotel rooms in each location. They both looked forward to the trip. He copied her in with the itinerary his travel agent had devised. 'But you've only booked one room in each city?' she queried. He had assumed too much. She broke all contact with him and blocked him online, following a terse email in which she accused him of disrespecting her as a friend, a woman and an artist. Once again, he realised his lust had made him cross an invisible line. A fool for lust.

CATALOGUE RAISONNÉ
OR THE CRUCIFIXION OF MAXIM J

He thinks it might be a form of insomnia but for months now he has been invariably waking up between 6.30 and 6.50 am. The morning beyond the blinds is still tentative and he always feels more tired than he felt when went to bed the previous evening, as if sleep had offered no succour. He is left awake with empty days ahead of him and deluged with the same thoughts. Of the kindness of women. Or, in some rare cases, their unkindness. He makes mental lists. Of those he knew. Of those he loved. Of those he didn't pay for. Of the anonymous ones he never knew the name of in the haste to couple. Christel. Catherine Guinard. Danielle Chamaillard. Maryann Armshaw. Lois Elizabeth Hough. Lora. Dawn T. The American tourist in Athens who silently left his hotel room at dawn. Jasmine Elaine T. Pamela L. Aida Kleivate, who came from Lithuania, but lived in Holland with another man. The Minneapolis bank executive who wore frayed underwear under her more elegant attire at the conference in St Louis, Minnesota. Liisa M. The pastor's wife from Baton Rouge, who complimented him on his girth. Kate C. Claudia Christiansen. Giulia Dezi. The story of his life. The map of his pain and sins.

THE ESPLANADE AT DESENZANO

It's a photograph taken barely a year after they married. She stands in profile on the esplanade at Desenzano, or it might have actually been an empty car park, just a few yards from Lake Garda. She looks so young and beautiful, slim in a simple summer dress, smiling, her blonde hair falling to her bare shoulders. It's an image that is indelibly imprinted on his mind, like the unforgettable sequence in Chris Marker's *La Jetée*, where for barely a second the still images come to life and a woman's face imperceptibly moves, comes alive and sharpens the enigma of the desperate story unfolding, providing it with abominable pathos and dread. The day in Desenzano was nowhere as dramatic. They had been visited by her elderly aunt from Brooklyn and were showing her the sights of Northern Italy, now that they lived there. He has searched everywhere for a copy of that photograph but can no longer locate it and it bothers him deeply, intent as he is to bring the past to life again, like a mad *Vermilion Sands* artist on a downhill spiral of private madness. That year, JG Ballard was still in the process of writing those striking stories. A few weeks later, they would travel to Venice for a trade conference where his London bosses would insist on visiting the casino on the Lido and she would initially be refused entry as the bouncer thought she was under-age, when she was actually 29. That evening was captured in another photo, where she is wearing her sleek purple wedding dress as they couldn't afford further evening wear at the time and it was the only suitable piece of attire in her limited wardrobe. He is beside her in his dark suit, looking stuck in time with the ridiculous sideburns he then had. He had always been years behind fashion. That photo now sits on the fireplace mantelpiece and it hurts him every time he catches sight of it, but he refuses to take it down. All the other colleagues and wives in the group shot are now dead he realises, as he was at the time the youngest of all the export team in the soft drinks division. It was in Desenzano, following her first ectopic pregnancy that she was mistakenly informed it was unlikely she would be able to bear children. So began a gallery of hospitals. A lump in her breast at the Royal Free. Reconstruction of her elbow and upper arm after she was hit by a car on a Shanghai street. Injections of steroids into her spine at Edgware General. And that was just the tip of the surface. Beauty attracts cruel retribution.

TURP

The prostate is a small gland in the pelvis found only in men. It is located between the penis and bladder, and surrounds the urethra (the tube that carries urine from the bladder out of the body). As a man gets older, the prostate may get bigger. This can put pressure on the bladder and urethra, and cause problems with passing urine, and in the worst scenario cause kidney failure due to the build-up of infectious waste inside the body. If medicines have not helped, you are offered surgery called a transurethral resection of the prostate (TURP). You are given a general anaesthetic, which means that you are asleep and do not feel any pain. The surgeon passes a thin tube called a resectoscope along your urethra until it reaches your prostate. This tube contains a light, camera and loop of wire. Your surgeon heats the loop of wire with an electric current and uses it to remove the section of your prostate causing problems. The pieces of removed prostate are looked at under a microscope to check that there are no abnormal cells. A small tube called a catheter then pumps liquid into your bladder and flushes away any remaining pieces of removed tissue. The TURP procedure can take up to one hour, depending on how much of your prostate is removed. In his case, it took four hours. He had been warned that even if the operation should prove successful, he would no longer be capable of discharging sperm again. He had not enquired about other consequences of the surgery in regard to his penis; the pain he was in superseded that curiosity alongside the indignity of wearing a catheter and a bag to collect his urine for a period of five months until they could schedule the operation. He was advised the next day that the material they had cut out of his prostate was benign, which was something of a relief although he was still pissing blood for a fortnight afterwards. It took him several weeks to tentatively verify that he could still achieve an orgasm, albeit without spillage and a distinct lack of hardness in his cock. Would this be the end of his career in sex? He raged at the prospect. Unwelcome thoughts submerged him: would he still achieve pleasure if he somehow rewired himself and consented to be sodomised by other men? Would they even find him attractive enough to want to fuck him? Would his remodelled prostate bear the brunt of repeated rectal assaults and ploughing? How long could he leave those questions unanswered?

REALITY LIES AT THE INTERSECTION
BETWEEN GRIEF AND THE IMAGINATION

There are thousands of beaches. He hasn't counted but, at a rough guess, he has probably set foot on the sands of between fifty and a hundred, equally divided between a variety of continents in his lifetime. And in the inner world he inhabits, every beach should have a story to tell. This is just one of them, broken into pieces, incoherent. Is it too much to ask the hypothetical readers to reassemble the shards? Concrete tower blocks loom in the distance and the colour of the sea shifts in cadence between grey and azure blue with sometimes flashes of green where the undertow reveals hidden depths in its wake. It has rained and the sand is wet. But the curtain of tropical rain finally parts and before the bathers, tourists and nudists can return to the fray, two massive silhouettes appear as the curtain of wet fog created by the caress of hot air against water lifts. A massive cruise ship and a submarine must have somehow crashed into each other close to the line of the coast, and washed up onto the shore, embedded in each other, like the skeleton of a prehistoric monster risen from the depths. It evokes Salvador Dali meets Godzilla. Passengers from the larger structure are frantically leaping from the height of their respective decks, an image that reminds him of the desperate jumpers of 9/11 throwing themselves into the void. But there is no sound: just like a silent movie. For a moment, he wonders if this is a film production in progress but he looks around and sees no camera, operators or directors conducting the apocalyptic scene. He is the only person present, aside from the cruise victims floundering out there, some still wading in the water and others stumbling across the sand in stop-motion, as he stands waist-high in the water of the infinity pool of his villa overlooking the beach, observing the scene in progress like an uninvolved spectator. Yesterday the waves out there had been unusually fierce and he had almost lost his spectacles when one had slammed into him sideways quite out of the blue when he was out swimming. Today the sea is calm. The cruise ship begins to disintegrate, folding into itself, impaled by the sleek copper-hued submarine. He is almost expecting to see a nuclear mushroom cloud rising in the distance above the sea in the direction of China. Or the advancing wall of a deadly *tsunami* tide rising towards the land. He looks around for his wife so they might run for safety from the incoming apocalypse. She is not there.

Also By The Terminal Press:

The J.G. Ballard Book 2013
Deep Ends: The J.G. Ballard Anthology 2014
Deep Ends: The J.G. Ballard Anthology 2015
Deep Ends: The J.G. Ballard Anthology 2016
Deep Ends: A Ballardian Anthology 2018
Deep Ends: A Ballardian Anthology 2019
Deep Ends: A Ballardian Anthology 2020
Deep Ends: A Ballardian Anthology 2021
Deep Ends: A Ballardian Anthology 2022
Deep Ends: A Ballardian Anthology 2023

Mike Bonsall - Ballardian Diversions

Dominika Oramus - Grave New World: The Decline of the West in
the Fiction of JG Ballard

Lawrence Russell - Radio Brazil
Lawrence Russell - Outlaw Academic
Lawrence Russell - Temple of the Two Moons

Paul A. Green - Terminal Transmissions

Don McKay - Gambari

Rick McGrath - Straight Man: Rock Star Interviews, Reviews &
Photos from the 1970s Underground Press
Rick McGrath - The Disenchanted Forest
Rick McGrath (editor) - Unauthorised Departures